JEALOUS

A THIN LINE BETWEEN LOVE AND HATE

TAWANA

CH

Jealous

Published by Mz. Lady P Presents

www.mzladypresents.com

ACKNOWLEDGMENTS

I asked Him to lead my steps and guide me to the right path I should be on in life and look where He brought me. Through Him all things are possible so I must thank my father God first and foremost. If you would have told me I would be the author of my first book in 2018 I probably would have laughed, yet here I am. I just finished my first book yall! Won't He do it!

I'm getting emotional as I prepare to acknowledge my support system. To all my sisters and brothers, I love you guys for believing in me and celebrating just as hard as I did when I learned that I would be writing a book. To my big brother Amentu a.k.a Lil Tee, who is currently finishing up his federal prison bid, you'll never know how much the wisdom you've gained and shared with me has impacted me. That one statement, "Sister you gone be good at whatever you do, but you got to find one thing and stick to it," changed me. If you know me, you know how many business ideas and ventures I was trying to start. My sister Sonyell, our prayer warrior, thanks for your inspiring words of encouragement. Lucy, my baby sister, whose middle name I used for one of my characters, thank you for reading the very first version of this book and wanting more! You read urban literature religiously and your advice and feedback meant the world to me. Travis, our talks about being successful and following our dreams also motivated me to push through this book. So, thanks for those talks! Crystal, my oldest sister, who sat with me through this whole process drinking coffee at no thirty in the morning listening to my ideas, I can't tell you how grateful I am to have you as my big sister. Thank you for watching my little baby Alani when I needed to beat these keys and she wouldn't let me be great. And my crazy niece, Ro-Ro, girl I'm going to make a character about you, you are a walking best seller! To my proud dad, Tiako, I know you're going to be smiling from ear to ear when you see your baby girls' name on the cover of her first book! Love you old man!

Tiffany Ramsey, I can't forget you! You were the very first person that I ever told about writing a book back when we were preteens in the projects, and you believed in me then. You were the first person to push me on the stage to perform my poetry. Thank you for always supporting me and believing in my talent.

My best friend Tierra, girl we had an adventurous teenage life and I wish we would've kept up with those darn notebooks! We'd have a few bestsellers on our hands..lbvs! Thank you for reading the first few chapters and telling me I had a page turner on my hands. Shout out to my mother's coworker, Jondalyn, who is an avid urban fiction reader; for reading the first few chapters and sending a threat through my mom for me to finish. Y´all don't know how much that positive feedback inspired me, so thanks!

To my pen sister and publisher, MzLadyP, you have by far been one of my biggest inspirations! Seeing you flourish over these years and push out book after book helped motivate me to start this journey. Thank you for believing in my writing skills and I look forward to taking over this industry with you!

Let's see, am I forgetting anyone? Just kidding, I saved the best for last; my queen, my backbone, my rock, the best mother in the world, Verlena Brown! For the last three years I've been trying to find my space in this crazy world. Refusing to go back to work because I believed in my talents, you have supported me through this journey. I know you didn't understand when I told you I don't want a job, because those bills wasn't letting up! But when I told you it was writing I would be pursuing this time, you finally gave me the blessing I've been wanting from you. "Baby this is your calling," were the words you said when you read those first few chapters and that meant the world to me. I love you lady!

My newest little miracle, Alani Jazmin, you are my motivation for everything I do, mommy loves you! If I forgot anyone, I apologize. Charge it to my head and not my heart.

IN LOVING MEMORY

In loving memory of my first born,
Tajane Shauntice Brown
2000-2016

SYPNOPSIS

Tramaine "Tray" Wallace is one of the biggest drug dealers in Chicago and is feared and respected by many. Having run a successful drug ring in one of Chicago's roughest projects, he is now rich, ready to retire from the drug game, focus on his legal business ventures, and find the right queen for his empire. That is until he learns that Manny, his right-hand man, is plotting to put him into retirement sooner than he planned.

Manny is fresh out of jail and ready to conquer the world with dreams of being rich. The only thing that's stopping him from running the city is his childhood friend Tray. Manny links up with his former cellmate, Romell, and plot to become the biggest dope boy Chicago has ever seen. Unbeknownst to Romell, Manny is about to get him involved in a territorial war.

Meet Monique, a product of her mom's prostitution who was neglected at a young age and forced to use her body to fend for herself and her younger sister. Desperate to escape the poverty and projects, she is ready to score a baller who will rescue her from her hard knock life. She thinks she finds that in Romell until he abruptly cuts her off. When her best friend, Amari, catches the eye of one of the neighborhoods biggest bosses, she becomes fueled with jealousy and anger and sets out to hurt and destroy any and every one in her path.

Amari, Monique's best friend, grew up sheltered by her parents and her only worry was bringing home good grades. After a devastating break up with her child's father, she finds herself partying with Monique to cope with her pain. Tray walks into her life and sweeps her right off feet. Oblivious to his thuggish lifestyle, she gets involved in a whirlwind of events that will drastically change her life.

Can Manny execute his plan and take over the city? Will Tray be able to retire or will his need for retaliation cause him to stay in the game until it's too late? Will Monique find the boss she's looking for or will jealousy and greed be her ultimate downfall?

Come with these intriguing characters on a roller coaster ride through the hoods of Chicago as their worlds collide and jealous ways force childhood friends to learn why it's a thin line between love and hate!

1

MONIQUE

He turned around and walked backed towards me slowly while puffing on the blunt. He stood right in front of me with his tall six -foot frame and blew the smoke in my face. "So, you threatening to call 12 on me?" He said as he snatched my cell phone from me and threw it on the floor so hard the glass screen shattered in a dozen pieces. The look in his eyes were so venomous I began feeling nauseous.

"What else I'm supposed to do Romell. I'm tired of you beating on me."

He took the blunt he had in his hand and used my face for his personal ashtray smashing the fire right into my jaw.

"Aaaagghh! What the fuck is your problem." I yelled as I grabbed my face to soothe the stinging sensation from the burn. Won't you just give me my key and get the fuck out."

Before I could utter another word, he punched me so hard I fell back on the loveseat. I felt my lip swell instantly. "Stupid bitch. I wish you would call the mufucking police on me."

Desperate to try and escape the ass whooping he was about to give me, I picked up a half empty Ciroc bottle and tried to bust his head wide open, it missed by an inch. He started throwing more punches at me. I picked up anything in my reach to try to inflict the pain on him that he was causing me. I put up a good fight too. He could barely handle my wild ass. "I'm keeping my baby." I yelled in between punches. You can't make me get no abortion."

"I might not be able to make you get no abortion from the doctor, but I'll beat this mufucka out of you." He said as grabbed me by my neck and flung me to the floor.

"Stop, let me go!" I broke free of his grasp and finally made it back on my feet. I tried to run but he kicked me in my back and I flew over the glass cocktail table shattering glass everywhere.

He rolled me over and choked me so hard I began to blank out. "With your tough smart mouth ass, what you gonna do now." He said as he tightened his grip around my neck. This bastard was trying to kill me. "*I hope...you fe feel like a...man..nnow.*" I mustered out barely breathing. That was the last thing I remember before I blanked out.

～

"PASS me that cup of water please." I was sitting in the county hospital once again for some shit this nigga done to me.

"How are you feeling? Are they about to release you?" He asked as if he really cared.

"How you think I'm feeling? You got what you wanted, I lost my baby." He didn't even reply. Just put his head down to avoid eye contact. I wasn't even excited about being pregnant, but I wasn't gonna have an abortion either. He said he wasn't ready for no more kids and I wasn't having that baby even if he had to beat it out of me. Romell showed up at the hospital with some balloons and candy apologizing like he always does after he beats me half to death. After I had come to, I was in the ER with police around my bed asking if I wanted to file domestic abuse charges. Of course, I knew better than to do that. If I rat on him I cut off my own food supply. Plus, things been different for me since I met him. I leave that crummy ass project apartment at least three times out the week to lamp up in his plush condo. I was now able to shop at Neiman Marcus and Macys instead of stealing from them. I was no longer relying on the CTA to get around because he gave me a new whip. Ain't no way I'm going back to my life the way it was before I met Ro.

We met a few months ago. I was at the corner store buying me a fifth of Remy and he walked up behind me and offered to pay for it. We exchanged numbers and he called me the same night. He came over and I gave the coochie up on the first night and he's been coming around ever since. Eventually he asked if he could pay me to make a few moves from my apartment and I happily obliged. Once the money started rolling in and he started to buy me all kind of expensive shit I decided I was gonna rock with him the long way. It doesn't hurt that he is fine as wine. He has full lips that complement the goatee and low fade he keeps freshly cut. He has caramel skin with a tall muscular frame and could dress his ass off. He was definitely pleasing to my eyes. So, I didn't care because he had abusive ways because I was finally fucking with a real nigga.

"You have another visitor." The nurse said as she walked in the room with my little sister, Kyra, stumbling behind her.

"Hey sis. You lost the baby?" She slurred out.

She was there when he was beating it out of me, so she should know. She was too busy getting drunk to even attempt to help me. Soon as she walked in the room it started smelling like nothing but liquor. She was sloppy drunk, and alcohol was coming out of her pores. "What you think?"

"Don't get no attitude with me, I'm not the one who did it. You need to direct that shit towards him." She laughed liked something was funny and pointed towards Romell.

She pulled the chair up to the side of the hospital bed and sat down like she was about to get comfortable. I needed to deal with him and did not need her nosey ass in my business. "Yo lil drunk ass didn't help. I would've never watched you get your ass beat. And I don't know what you sitting down for, I'll see you at home."

Romell butt in, "She knew better."

"Shut up Romell, ain't nobody talking to you."

Kyra got up to leave. "Here yall go, you about to get your ass whooped at the hospital. You oughta be glad he did beat it out of you cause you bout didn't know who the daddy was anyway."

"Bitch get the fuck out my room, I know whose baby that was. SECURITY!" I was pissed the fuck off, I wanted to jump up and beat her ass, but I had lost too much blood and was weak as hell. Plus, I didn't want to clown and get kicked out the hospital. That's why I hate a drunk bitch, she would've never said that shit if she was sober. She gets on my last nerve, bitch don't have no life, no friends and always drunk. She's just like our sorry ass mother. I had been taking care of her since I was eleven years old, the day our mother walked out our two-bedroom low income apartment and left us to fend for ourselves. She came and went as she pleased, but more often than not we were home alone with no food, no clothes, and no love. Crack cocaine became her top priority and she chased that high daily. I tried my best with my sister but what could I teach her when I was a baby myself. We were only five years apart. The stress of life got to her and she turned to the bottle and never looked back. I sympathized with her and did my best to raise her because she didn't ask to be dealt the cards she was dealt. I tried to keep a tight leash on her because I wanted her to have more out of life, but once she became a teenager she started feeling herself and felt like she no longer had to respect me. Even though she gets on my nerves and stay pissing me off, I still kept her close and made sure she was good because she's the only family I got.

"Don't pay her drunk ass no attention. She don't know what the fuck she talking about." I said trying to erase what Kyra said out of his thought process.

"Drunk people speak sober thoughts." He replied nonchalantly. "I don't know what you be doing when I'm not around."

"If that's the case why you still fucking on me?"

"Because I like the way you suck my dick" He said grabbing his pants. His disrespect had no boundaries.

"Yeah okay." I said dismissing his ignorance.

"What you tell the police. I know you didn't give them pigs my muthafucking name."

"You'd be in handcuffs already if I did." I remarked snidely as I rolled my eyes.

I was never gonna call the police in the first place. I just wanted him to leave me alone about having my baby. Besides, he always hit me when I asked too many questions or when I was late meeting him at the exact time he requested. Hell, he hit me whenever he felt like it. He choked me, slapped me, kicked me, and committed any other act of domestic violence he could think of. But I didn't care because he had changed my life. I'm too rebellious to obey all his rules though. So even if it meant getting my ass beat from time to time, I will always get flip at the lip. That lil shit he be doing don't really hurt me anyway. Life and the streets have been whooping my ass for so long that I'm immune to pain.

2

TRAY

"What's up Manny. How does it feel to be a free man again?" I asked as soon as he walked up to the car. I had been sitting with two of the guys waiting for my right-hand man to be released from jail. He was just finishing up a case he caught for murdering his uncle.

"It's a feeling I can't even explain. Just the idea of looking up at the dark sky tonight is making me emotional. It feels good to walk without those shackles on my feet and without my hands cuffed."

"Shit we take for granted everyday huh?"

"The littlest things man. I could go on all day, but a nigga need some real food. I don't want to taste another noodle or eat another gatdamn bean for the rest of my life."

"What's up my nigga. I ain't seen you since I was making mud cakes in front of the building." Fendi said as he got out the front seat of the car and greeted Manny with our signature handshake.

The handshake was created years ago by the original gangstas of our neighborhood, Bricksquare projects, one of the worse neighborhoods in the city. It was how all the G's and hustlas greeted each other. Manny was smiling from ear to ear as he hopped in the passenger seat. "What's the word Fendi, yea it's been eleven years and you was a bad ass project kid when I left running around kicking on people doors and shit. But I see you doing big boy thangs now, y'all out here eating." He looked at the custom interior and observed the quality in the diamonds everybody was rocking and could tell our team was doing big things. "When I left you was driving a putt putt that you could hear coming up the road from a mile away. Now you pull up on a nigga in a custom Tesla with rollies on and shit." He said looking at me with a big ass smile on his face.

Damn it felt good to have my dog back home. I missed his crazy ass. He was always cracking jokes. The man should've been a comedian. In grade school, he was the ultimate class clown. His mother was at the school every other week in meetings about his "behavior problems" as the teachers would say. Me and this nigga come from the dirt together. Our mothers were friends, so we started playing together as snot nosed toddlers. Being that we both were our moms only sons, we grew up more as brothers than friends. Whenever you saw him, you saw me. We were both influenced by Chuck, he was running the hood back then. We aspired to be like him because coming from our neighborhood, you had to be a dope boy to get the money and the respect. Manny used to always say we would take over Bricksquare projects when we got older and then eventually conquer the whole windy city. Two years before we graduated from grade school, his mom went to prison and he became very withdrawn. He had to move in with his sick grandmother and he hated to have to leave the neighborhood. After graduation, he killed his uncle and had been in jail ever since. He never told me why he killed him, just that he deserved to die.

Before he went to jail we was both lil boys out here selling nicks and dimes, but shit was different now. I got on and made sure my whole team ate. And even though he had been gone all those years, I made sure his commissary was good every month. "Yea, we out here living our best life. And now that you back, it's time for you to upgrade your lifestyle too. First things first, your favorite gun." I said as I reached under the seat and pulled out a shiny new Smith and Wesson.

Manny rubbed his hands together in anticipation to hold his favorite toy. "Now this what the fuck I'm talking about." He said taking the gun and caressing it like he wanted to make love to it. "It's time for me to earn my stripes."

I opened the glove compartment where I put his new Rolex, diamond earrings, and a custom chain with black diamonds. I passed him the jewelry bag and his eyes lit up with excitement. "Welcome home bro."

"Damn. How much money you getting? This shit had to cost a grip." He said as he took the rollie out the case and closely examined the diamonds.

By now we were on the highway headed back to the city. I had Choppa to stop by the mall, so we can get Manny out that jail uniform. I bought him a whole wardrobe with shoes for almost every outfit. "Nigga you need to go in one of these stalls and put one of those joints on now. That prison gear is an eyesore."

"Man, I make these jogging pants look good. It look better than that corny ass suit you got on. Who the fuck are you now, James Bond or something?"

Choppa and Fendi found that shit funny as hell as they erupted in laughter. "I'm a business man, fuck you mean. I've outgrown all those clothes with labels plastered all over em and shit. I'll still rock a pair of mikes every now and then. But this me now Manny, suits and dress shoes."

"Get your young old ass outta here. What's up with a barbershop. I look like wolf man."

"That's our next stop."

∽

"You might as well get ready to come off that cash, Golden State taking they ass home this year." Manny said as he looked at the ninety-inch screen that occupied a whole wall of the barbershop.

"Man get the fuck out of here. The Warriors about to send those boys home crying. They gone blow they ass out tonight." We were getting linings and haircuts while catching up on the playoffs. I put my money on Curry and the Warriors because I know they will be getting in Cleveland ass in the finals.

"Don't count those boys out. They came to play ball." Manny continued. "And even if they make it through the first few games, King James will be handing out ass whoopings on a platter in the last games of the finals."

"Yall mufuckas gone stop underestimating greatness. That boy Steph Curry is a beast." I replied as I motioned the loctician over.

"Who you got your money on Fendi?"

"Yall already know I'm just waiting for Cleveland to warm up so Lebron can show all his haters why he being labeled as one of the greatest to ever do it."

"Yall niggas love riding Lebron dick. The man is an average player at best."

"Average? Get the fuck outta here. Ain't no player in the game today better than him. Numbers don't lie my nigga. Betting against him is like donating to charity. You just giving your money away." Fendi added.

"How long it's gonna take to twist me up?" I asked the sexy loctician as soon as she walked up. She was the only female in the barbershop, but she was cold with the braids and dread locs. I was in her chair every week getting my locs freshly twisted. "Put your money where your mouth is then. I got $2500 on Golden State."

Fendi cupped his mouth and then let out a sarcastic chuckle. "Aight, but you might as well pay me now."

"I don't even got $2500 but I want in on this bet." Manny added. "That's easy money."

"Nigga you'll have it by the time the playoffs over. Let's do it." I challenged Manny. "What you got on this bet?" I asked Choppa who was sitting at the booth next to me quietly receiving a fresh line up.

"Fuck all those niggas. I ain't putting my money on none of they ass. Until Chicago get a star player for our team, this shit just pure entertainment. I can't root for nobody but my home team and we haven't had a reason to cheer since the mufucking 90's." Choppa said totally uninterested in the whole debate.

After we were done at the barbershop, I had one last stop to make. Choppa and Fendi had to go back to the hood to check in on the workers. Meanwhile, I hung out with Manny.

"I can tell her ass big even under that long ass coat." Manny said watching a lady strut by. He damn near twisted his neck off turning around in his seat watching her until she was out of his eyesight. "Where the hoes at? You should've had some bitches in the car with you instead of those lil niggas."

"Those the lil homies, they been helping me hold shit down. But it's plenty of fish out here."

"And I'm ready to filet they ass."

"These bitches don't even got no standards out here no more bro. A drink and a high and they just giving the pussy away. I know you ready to go dive head first in you some."

"Hell yeah, somebody about to get their black blown the fuck out."

"You better strap up, your ass will definitely be shooting out babies in the first bitch you nut in."

"Naw nigga, I ain't popping out no shorties no time soon. I'm tryna get to this money out here."

"That shit don't always work, just don't get caught out here lacking. Shit is different now. Remember when hoes used to give us a hard time because our paper wasn't long enough?" He nodded his head at the memory. "Well these hoes throwing the pussy at me now. But I don't want none of they money hungry ass. I need me a real queen."

"I'll take a few money hungry hoes with a side of ratchet bitches please. I can just smell the pussy now." He said with the cheesiest grin on his face.

I laughed and reached inside the cupholder and pulled out a key. "This right here is your chic magnet." I said passing him the key as we pulled up to the back of the house where I had his new car parked.

"Awwwww shit." He said as he unhooked his seatbelt and hit the alarm on the new black on black six series 2018 BMW I got for him.

He was about to hop out the car, but I stopped him. "Slow down bro. I got one more thing for you." I passed him a cell phone with all the proper connects already programmed in it.

"How the fuck you work this thing? Where is the power button?" He asked while examining the iPhone 8 like it was a foreign object.

"I'll explain all that." I said laughing at the idea of him being damn near a caveman. Technology had evolved tremendously in the eleven years he'd been incarcerated. "For now, all you need to know how to do is make and receive calls. This is the power button." I said explaining the basics. "Everything else you'll learn as you go."

"Aight. This has been one hell of a welcome home. I can't thank you enough for everything." He was starting to get emotional.

"Don't be going cotton on me. I told you I was out here running shit. And as long as I'm good, you good. But these streets need you. Fendi and Choppa been doing a lot of major shit for me at Bricksquare. You were the missing piece to the puzzle and now that you're home, you gotta show people how a real bricksquare gangsta do shit. You gone run the buildings for now and they will be working under you. I barely go to the hood, so you will be my eyes and ears from now on. So, go get knee deep in you some pussy and hit my phone tomorrow." I said while passing him $10,000. "This should hold you over until you get your first payout for working. Meanwhile, I'm gonna holla at the team to let them know a real nigga done touched down and you will be sliding through."

He took the money and put it inside is back pocket. "Bricksquare gangstas for life." He said as we did our handshake before he exited the car.

"BSG fo life."

3

ROMELL

They need to hurry the fuck up and release her. I got a big ass shipment that I need her to be available for. I don't know why she always running her dumb ass to the hospital. The same shit they using to clean and patch her ass up with they sell at Walgreens. She claims her sister called the ambulance soon as I left that day but this bitch lying. She came up here on purpose. She probably thought I was gonna react to her sister's comment about not knowing who she was pregnant by. But I let that shit roll off my back because I don't care who baby that hoe was carrying. She thinks I don't know about her background because I'm not from her hood but Manny told me all about her ass. I usually only let her suck my dick or I use a rubber, but I did slip up one day about two months ago and hit it raw. That's why I beat that baby outta her, it was a possibility it was mines and ain't no way I was letting her go through with that shit.

"Look I need you out of here, when are they releasing you? You been in here for three days already."

"I just lost a baby and thanks to you I'm bleeding from my coochie, my face, and my arm. Did you think they would release me the same day?"

"You done had worse shit done to you than losing a baby and getting a few stitches. They just trying to milk that medical card. But they interfering with my plans. It's a big shipment on the way and you need to be there to pick it up." I said as I handed her a piece of paper with an address written on it. Before Manny came home from jail he had me to establish this bullshit ass relationship with her so things would already be in motion when he was released. He put me up on her because he said she was a hustler who fucked, sucked, and did anything for some cash. He joked about how he taught her how to suck dick at a very young age.

"Could you at least give me time to heal before you start making demands?"

Aside from losing her baby, she had a large shard of glass embedded in her arm when she landed on that table. It was a deep wound and she had to get it stitched up. I knew she was in pain and hurt over losing her baby, but I could give a fuck less, I needed shit done. I ignored her question and continued giving her instructions. "Once the shipment comes, take it there." I had just got my hand on some major weight. I been small timing too long and this one is about to change me and my people lives forever. I been finessing the neighborhood whore to get a lot of shit done through her. I needed my whole team on the streets and couldn't risk nobody getting caught or nothing being traced back to us. Monique has been the perfect pawn, a money hungry bitch with nothing to lose. But once this shipment is in and setup, I'm done using her trifling ass.

"That's fucked up Romell. You come with here with balloons and shit like you're really sorry for what you did when you don't give a fuck do you?"

"Of course, I care baby." I said as I got up and got all in her personal space and whispered in her ear. "But if they don't release you by the morning you better walk out this bitch or I'm coming to get you myself. You got work to do."

~

THE NEXT DAY I went to Bricksquare projects to get the package from Monique's crib. As usual they raggedy ass elevators wasn't working and I had to take the stairwell through these pissy ass hallways all the way up to the ninth floor.

Just as she was told she released herself from the hospital and handled that business. I walked through the door of her small two-bedroom apartment and she was lying on the couch sleep. Her arm was patched up and she had on nothing but her panties, bra and the hospital socks.

"Monique. Wake up." I was outta breath gasping for air from walking all those flights of stairs. I made a mental note to cut back on smoking because that shit is taking a toll on my lungs.

"It's in my room on the side of the bed." She responded without even opening her eyes.

I could tell she was still irritated about having to release herself from the hospital but as long as she did what I needed her to do, she could be irritated all she want to. Bitches like her are only good for what she's good for and that's nothing.

"Get your ass up and go get it and bring it to me." I demanded as I plopped down on the sofa chair and tried to catch my breath. "And bring the scale back with you."

"Damn. Can I at least get some rest. I don't have no energy."

"You don't get paid to lamp around, now go do what the fuck I said." I don't know why she was testing my patience.

"I did what I get paid for. And you being in here using my crib is what I get paid for." She said still not budging.

I reached over to the couch she was laying on and grabbed a handful of her hair and jerked her neck so hard she fell off the couch. "Now get up and do what I said before you be back in the emergency room."

She came back with the scale and the work and threw it on the sofa then walked back in her bedroom and slammed the door. I picked up the box and sliced thru it with a razor blade and the contents of it damn near made my dick hard. All I saw was dollar signs as I pulled the bricks out of the box. I been waiting a long time to score this amount of dope and it was finally time to take over this city. When I went to jail my whole team fell off without me out here. But now that I'm back on, it's time for everybody that ever showed me loyalty to get put on.

"What's up Black?"

"Whaddup my nigga. I've been waiting all day for this phone call." I could tell he was smiling through the phone.

"I can tell because I'on even think I heard this mufucka ring before you answered."

"Man it's been rough out here and I knew once you got that package, shit gone start being different."

"So that means you ready?"

"Nigga I was born ready."

"Well I definitely got that package, so you can gone ahead and put the team together." Black was my A1. He's the reason I was getting money on the southside. Even though I'm not from Chicago, he had introduced me to the right people that allowed me to make a few moves. Shit was dry in their area before I put niggas on, so it was easy to take over.

"We just waiting for you to bring it."

"Aight, I gotta make another stop so I should be over there in about a hour or two."

"10-4." He replied before ending the call.

I picked up the remote to the TV and turned to ESPN. I decide to get my sports fix while I put this shit together. I needed to ship some to my people out of town, get Black moving on the south side, and connect with my nigga Manny. Manny got shit on lock on this side of town and I been waiting for this ever since I came home. I was so glad he was finally out of jail so we can join forces and become the biggest dope boys Chicago has ever seen.

4

MANNY

*ne month later.....*

THIS SHIT IS GOING BETTER than I expected. My nigga Ro really came through. We about to take over this whole fucking city. I been working under Tray since I came home and I appreciate him looking out for me. But I spent a lot of nights in my cell imagining what it would be like to take over and I can't be the boss if I'm working under another nigga. Tray is only in that position because I wasn't here to get it. I vowed to myself that I wasn't gonna risk my freedom to make another nigga rich. I met Romell a few years ago when I was finishing up my bid down state. We were cellies and was always talking about getting money. He told me he was gonna score a big ass shipment when he got out and strictly outta loyalty he was gonna look out for me. He was released before me and stayed true to his word. That nigga really came through. He started me off with ten bricks, all butta. I had my shit moving through Tray's operation and shit was running smooth and incognito. "How much we got left?" I was meeting with my lil nigga Duke to see how shit was going out there with our work.

"We still got four bricks left."

"Why the fuck it's still so much? We run a twenty-four hour operation so that shit should be gone by now."

"Because we still gotta move Tray shit too. Especially if you don't want him on to what the fuck we doing. That nigga will kill us both."

"Fuck Tray. I ain't worried about him." I only put Duke under my wing because he reminded me of me. He was hungry and would grind by any means necessary. This lil nigga never slept because our philosophy is real hustlas never sleep. I was still grooming him because he was only 19. But with my guidance, he will be prepared for anything these streets throw at him. It seems like he about to fold on me though. I know stepping on Tray's toes is playing Russian roulette with my life. Everybody who's somebody in this city knows who Tray is. He is like the God of the streets to these lil niggas. But all of that is about to change and this lil nigga can't fold on me now. "I put you on my team cuz you my lil homie and I thought you had a lotta heart so don't go soft on me now. I'm giving you the opportunity to get you and your family out the hood. Tray pulling up to big ass mansions every night and you worried about that nigga while you crammed up in this two-bedroom apartment with your whole family."

"It'll change my life If I make it out alive. I think I want out before he's on to us. I got kids to live for Manny."

I acted like I didn't hear his last statement. "I'll be back tomorrow to meet with you for the money off what you got and I'm gonna be dropping more work off." He cut me off like he was about to say something else, so I stopped him midsentence to let him know how critical this is to his life. "Mrs. Reed at Adult Day Care today right?" He nodded his head in agreement as I asked the next questions. "Your kids go to school right off 63rd and Drexel, your babymama work at Target, and your only other family lives in Gary, Indiana right?" I asked him as I pulled my Smith and Wesson from my waist and blew into the barrel.

"Yea why?" He asked as sweat beads started to form on his forehead.

"I would hate to take my favorite gun to any one of those places and pay them a visit." I emphasized by aiming at his family picture with my gun. At this point he no longer had an option. Shit was going too good now and ain't no way he was stopping. He'd witnessed me put bullets through many men in broad daylight, so he knew I'd take out his whole family with no hesitation.

"WHAT's up with the money JD?" Tray had asked me to meet up with him to get the 50k he turned up short on last week. He said the building got hit and they took everything. Tray usually let shit like that slide but nobody else knows about it and nobody else took a loss. So, this nigga scheming according to Tray and he wanted his cash. It was time to pay the piper.

"I'm still working on it. I told you the police took everything and our work been moving slow. I need at least another week."

Another week was way too long. That shit is interfering with what I'm trying to do. I don't give a fuck about his sympathy story, it was time to pay up. "How much you got so far?" He reached inside his pocket and passed me $32,000. "Times up." I put the silencer on my gun and shot him between his eyes before putting in a call to Tray. *"Hello. He said he need another week."*

"Aight, get whatever he got now and give him another week, not a day longer."

"He said he didn't have nothing for me yet." I said as I counted the money he'd just given me.

5

TRAY

I been running Bricksquare for almost ten years now and they have made me rich. I was born and raised in those buildings. Back in the early 2000's when I was graduating from grade school, the crack era was booming. My mother had tried her best to keep me out the streets, but it was inevitable. I had seen so many hungry nights and was tired of seeing her struggle. I finished high school to make her proud, but it was only for her. I had no interest in school. I'd gotten my first taste of drug money at the age of eleven and haven't looked back since. I started out nickeling and diming like the average young boy from the hood, but I figured shit out quick. The president of the drug ring at Bricksquare, Chuck, had seen my grind and hunger and put me right under his wing. He taught me everything about the game and eventually put me in charge of the workers. I went from selling bags to pushing ounces in a matter of months. Before being indicted by the feds in 08, he passed me the torch and I been running the square ever since.

So much had changed since Chuck was running shit. He only dealt crack, dope, and weed. These young niggas listening to these rappers and getting high off all kind of shit these days. So, I tapped into every addicts drug. I had leaf, crack, dope, pills, and weed. I even thought about getting syrup since Lil Wayne and Future got these young niggas drinking dirty sprite. But I didn't like what it was doing to my people. I know that sounds fucked up because I supply the other shit, but that was already going on before I got in the game. I just didn't want to be the one to introduce my hood to that shit. After I got off the phone with Manny I had my baby mama, Ivory, to come and pick me up. She pulled up in her 2017 silver Range with tinted windows. A gift I had got for her 26th birthday last year. I called her because I wanted to pay the hood a visit and stay low key. Some things haven't been adding up lately. Although I had niggas in place to make sure shit was moving and operating like it should, I didn't trust anyone, man or woman. That's another valuable lesson Chuck taught me at an early age.

Riding around the hood everything looked normal. Customers were coming and going as usual. Even though it was cold as hell outside, niggas was still huddled in front of the building shooting dice. While riding pass the building I had my crack in, 2103, I spotted an unfamiliar face going in. I knew everybody from this neighbor-hood and he definitely not from over here. "Park in the back of the lot." I instructed her and sent her to find out who this nigga is. All she had to do was walk pass him and she got his attention. My baby mama is definitely bad. A red head with light skin and hazel brown almond shaped eyes. With an hour glass figure and a cute smile, she's my savage Lisa Raye.

"It's cold as heck out today right." Ivory said to the stranger as they waited for the elevator.

"Yea it is. Where yo man at shorty?"

"I don't have one of those."

"You too cute for some nigga not to have you on lock. Where that nigga you fucking?"

"See now you getting too personal. I ain't fucking with nobody or fucking nobody cuz all you niggas got a one track mind." She kept the conversation going until they got on the elevator. She waited for him to press his floor and pressed for the floor above. After waiting for him to get off, she stood in the elevator shaft until the door closed.

She watched the apartment he went to and darted down the stair-well. "His name is Romell a.k.a. "Ro" and he went to apartment 906." She said as she got back in the truck.

"Take me to my car." I instructed her.

"But you said we was finna hang out all day today Tray." She whined while pulling off.

Besides being the mother of my child, she was also my bad bitch. She been down for me since day one. Anything I needed done she was there without question. If I needed some disrespectful hoes handled, she and her crew took care of it. She would make trips out of town to cop work for me, register my guns in her name, the whole nine. Plus, she gives head like no one I've ever met. That's why she doesn't want for anything. I fuck her every now and then to keep her happy but that's as far as it will ever go. She always pressing me about a relationship but she not who I want as a wife. "Something just came up that needs to be handled."

"I'm horny as fuck, as least give me some dick first." She said while caressing my penis.

"Pay attention to the road." I was becoming irritated with her thirstiness.

"It's cool, I can get dick elsewhere." She could've kept that shit to herself. I bet not catch whatever nigga she fucking and she damn sure bet not bring em around my son. Even though I don't want a relation-ship with her, she still my bitch.

6

MONIQUE

We pulled up to club essence and exited the car. I was looking like a snack with my ice washed ripped Levi shorts. I complemented them with a red bra covered by a white netted shirt. I rocked my favorite red Steve Madden pumps. With my red lipstick, gold accessories and 24-inch Malaysian hair falling down my back, you couldn't tell me I wasn't the baddest bitch walking in the club. I dragged my friend Amari out with me because she needed to get her homebody ass out the house. She wore a simple ass backless silver Versace dress with some red bottoms. She'd spent an arm and a leg on her outfit and I still looked better than her. She wore her hair in a high ponytail with a Chinese bang. She was even rocking her mink lashes, now I wish I would've got mine done.

After waiting in that long ass line for about 45 minutes, we were finally entering the doors of Club Essence. Even though it was the dead of the winter, girls in Chicago still dressed half naked going out and I was freezing my ass off. This is one of my favorite spots because only ballers and celebrities frequented this club. Lawd knows I need me a few stiff drinks after having my baby beat outta me. We made our way to the top floor to grab a table by the VIP section. I held our spot at the table while Amari went to the bar to get our drinks.

"Let me get a tequila sunrise and a bahama mama." Amari said to the bartender.

"Put that on my tab." A man said from behind her.

Amari declined the offer. "I'm cool, I got my own money." Amari said as she reached in her Versace clutch to get her debit card.

"Okay, I'll take that. But I'll see you again." The stranger with freshly twisted locs said as he winked and walked off.

"Damn you took all day." I yelled as soon as she walked to the table. I had popped me a pill and needed my drink to go with it.

"Some dude damn near wouldn't let me leave the bar without paying for our drinks. And you know how that shit goes, they pay for your drink and follow you around all night thinking you owe them something."

I had to laugh at her for that. My friend needs to get out more often. She so stuck in the early 2000s it's ridiculous. "Girl these days you better be glad a nigga offer to pay for your drink, these dudes be expecting you to pay for their drinks. Did you at least get his name?" I asked as I sipped my tequila.

"I think he said Tray. I couldn't really hear him over this loud ass music."

I almost spit my drink out. This dumb hoe had just turned down a drink offer from one of the most paid niggas in Chicago. I popped another pill to further intoxicate myself. I had to get myself right because the club scene is my job. I always caught some thirsty nigga willing to trick some cash at the end of the night and I had to be intoxicated so I could be numb to my surroundings and actions. And if that was Tray that Amari saw, I'm about to give that nigga the best head of his life tonight. Romell done gave me a small taste of what having some money feels like so I'm trying to play in the major league from here on out. Plus, that bastard been acting funny ever since he picked up that big ass package. He even went so far as to get his number changed. "I would've let his ass pay for it." I grabbed Amari to drag her to the dance floor with me. "Can yall please make sure nobody take our seats." I asked the strangers who had joined us at the table. *Toot toot....girl I wanna see you twerk* blared through the speakers and I tore the floor up off my song. After that song went off we went back to our table to find a gold bottle waiting for us. "Who sent this?" The people at the table said it came from V.I.P. I stood up and looked towards the V.I.P door and one of the security guards motioned for us to come over. The guard led us through the exclusive area. It is gorgeous back here. Several chaise lounge chairs were strategically placed throughout the room and each of them were occupied by half naked women. There were smoke black floor to ceiling windows that overlooked the whole club. You could see everything and everybody moving in this bitch. The guard pointed to a table in the corner of the room and told us that's who sent for us. It was definitely Tray, the man of my wettest dreams. He was finally ready to give me a chance. I'd kick every nigga I'm fucking with to the curb without a second thought to get with him. "Hey Tray." I said in my sexiest voice.

"Monica right?" He responded distractedly.

"MO-NIQUE remember?" I'd only introduced myself to him a dozen times. He could at least remember my damn name.

"Oh yea, that's right. But who is your friend. She sexy as hell." He asked me while looking at Amari.

"Why don't you ask her I said with an attitude." This is the part I don't miss about hanging out with her, she be getting all my attention. And this is the wrong time for that.

"That's him, the one that was offering to pay for our drinks." She said to me with irritation in her voice then turned around to him. "My name is Amari and didn't I tell you I wasn't interested in you buying me a drink."

"Don't be so feisty cutie."

"I see you just don't take no for an answer do you? Or are you just used to getting what you want?"

"A little bit of both." Tray replied with an arrogant tone. Tray is the epitome of a sex symbol. The man is cut like you wouldn't believe. He has nice full soft looking lips that complement his neatly trimmed goatee. He has mesmerizing teddy bear like eyes and the prettiest white teeth. His shoulder length dreads were always freshly twisted.

When he smiles, I could just get lost in his dimples. Damn, my stuff is throbbing just looking at him.

"Well just like I told you earlier, I'm not interested." Amari said as she passed him the gold bottle and left the table. "She just tripping because she's still in love with her babydaddy." I was trying to say anything to get his attention off her and on me.

"Oh, she got a man?" Tray asked as he watched Amari walk away until she was out the club.

Amari was short and cute. She stands about 5"1 and is petite yet curvaceous with perky breasts and a nice sized butt. Her high yellow complexion and light grey eyes came courtesy of her half European father. So, I understood why he was so mesmerized by her, but that bitch ain't all that.

I'd finally said something that got his attention. "Yea she do, but I don't. And you know I been checking for you for a minute now. You used to tell me I was too young, but I'm grown now, real grown." I purred as I scooted closer to him. He didn't even answer me. He just slid the bottle towards me and left the table. I told Amari she could leave without me. I left the club with Quan, a dude from the square I was always able to get money from. He was willing to trick off his pack money and I was willing to take it. We went to a lil sleazy motel on Cicero avenue, drank the bottle of Ace of Spade, and fucked for a little while. I didn't give him no head because he wasn't paying enough. When I woke up sober I was immediately ready to go. How the fuck I wind up in bed with this bum again when I was supposed to strike gold last night. Ugh.

7

ROMELL

W hat's up big homey?" Me and Manny met up at one of his spots out west. Everything went so smooth with the first shipment. Monique did her part before I cut her thot ass off. Now all we had to do was get rid of the rest. I needed to pay back the plug, so I had no time to waste.

"Whaddup my nigga. You really came through." Manny said as he puffed on a black and mild. I hate the way that shit smell.

"You thought I was bullshitting, didn't you?" It's not every day that a young nigga like me get their hands on the amount of dope I got. Before I could say something else a young nigga came out the only room that was in the apartment. I instantly upped my burner. "Nigga you ain't tell me nobody else was gonna be here. The fuck yall tryna do? Set me up?"

"Chill bro, you know you my dude and I ain't on no fu shit like that." He said calming me down. "This my lil nigga Duke. He part of the team that's helping me push this weight. I wanted him to meet the man that's changing his life."

I put my gun back in my pants while introducing myself to Duke. He looked kinda nervous and unsure of himself. I picked that up within the first two minutes of meeting him. He kept looking around at the money and the dope pacing back and forth between the window and the couch. But he's Manny's problem. As long as they make that money back, I ain't gotta deal with lil dude. I picked up the money I came for and dropped off more bricks before leaving out the door.

Since I was in the area, I decided to stop by Monique crib. I figured I'd get my dick sucked before I go back to the house.

"What you doing here?" She asked as I walked in the door with the key I still had. She was in the kitchen cooking, so I was right on time.

"I came to see you, don't act like you ain't happy to see me." She was blowing my number up before I got it changed.

"You got a lot of muthafucking nerve coming up in here acting like I'm supposed to be jumping off the walls because you walked through the door. I'm glad you think you can just cut me off like that."

I don't know who the fuck she think she talking too. She lucky I'm too tired to go upside her head right now. "Man just fix me a plate." She looked sexy as hell standing over that stove in that silk gown. It stopped right above her butt, just enough to expose her checks. Mo had ass for days with a small waist to go with it. Caramel complexion with dark brown eyes. She could get down in the kitchen and could suck a mean dick. If she wasn't such a slut, she'd make a good woman. But I'm not into turning hoes into housewives. After I finished my plate, I tried to fuck her in the mouth, but she was resisting like a muthafucka.

"Boy let me go, I'm cramping and I'm just not in the mood for your shit today. So, if you're gonna beat my ass go ahead and get it over with cuz I'm not about to suck your dick. And you still ain't telling me why the fuck I haven't heard from you."

"Ain't nobody finna do nothing to you, just calm down and come here." She was on some garbage because I don't care how mad she got at me, she'd never deprive me of a nut. But I don't give a fuck about her attitude. Even though the food she cooked was fye, I didn't come over here for no damn meal."

"Either you gonna force me to do it or you can get out my face."

She walked in her room and came back out fully dressed. She was being blatantly disrespectful, but I was already tired, and that meal didn't make it no better. She walked right out the door slamming it hard as fuck behind her. She was big mad.

"What the fuck was that?" Monique's little sister, Kyra, said running out of her room.

Her hair was tousled all over her head and she was wearing a sports bra and boy shorts. She wasn't built up like Mo but her athletic stature and cute face reminded me of Laila Ali. "Your sister slamming doors and shit like she done lost her damn mind." I was still admiring her deep dimples and natural beauty.

"Yall always fighting." She walked into the kitchen to get a bottle of water. She was a mini alcoholic and that liquor kept her dehydrated. "At least she cooked before you pissed her off." She said while lifting the tops to see what was in the pots.

"Come here Kyra." I was no longer able to resist her. She was the exact opposite of her sister. She didn't party or do half the things Mo does. She's a good girl with the exception of her drinking problem. Mo even mentioned to me that at 17 years old, she's still a virgin. I'm about to change that though. That bitch didn't want to give me no head so now I'm finna get some pussy from her sister.

"What boy?" She asked while walking towards me.

There was never a time when she was all the way sober, so I know this finna be easy. All she need is some attention. Her sister so scared she gonna turn out like her, so she keeps her under lock and key. "Boy? Does a boy have a dick like this?" I asked while exposing all 8 inches.

"Romell!" She covered her mouth with a surprised look on her face. She act like she just saw a ghost. "You better put that back in your pants." She said while reaching behind the picture frame to grab her bottle of exclusive vodka. She drank right out the bottle. That's the most unlady like shit ever.

"Don't be scared lil lady, it doesn't bite. Touch it." By now my dick was rock hard at the thought of getting some of that virgin pussy. I stood over her and massaged my rock hard piece. "I got something for you, let's go in your room." She was trying so hard to resist. But with a little more persistence and another shot of vodka, I was about to have my way.

"If you don't get out my face and put your dick back in your pants." I completely ignored her and lifted her off the couch. I carried her to her room with my dick slinging and tossed her on the bed. She was still holding on to that damn bottle. I pulled her to the edge of the bed and snatched her boy shorts off. I was rough yet gentle and she was no longer putting up a fight. I can tell her little pussy ain't been touched because I had to pull her lips apart to find her clitoris. I started sucking on that pretty little pussy, something I'd never done to Monique. She tasted better than I imagined and when she let out her first moan, I knew I had her. I teased her clit with my tongue and inserted a finger inside her. Her shit tight as fuck. I ain't fucked a virgin since I was one. She started to grind her hips as she enjoyed the feel of my mouth. Once I got her juices flowing, I went in for the kill. She spread her legs open wanting it now more than me. "I'm a virgin Romell so please be gentle and take it slow." I had to force my dick inside of her and the tightness caught me off guard. I busted instantly. "Damn baby. I need another round. I didn't know it was about to feel that good."

I PULLED in the back of the building to meet with Manny and Duke again. The past few weeks they pushed a lot of weight and I needed to drop off more. When I got to the parking lot, I noticed Duke standing in front of his car with loud ass music on trying impress the hoes that were standing around him. Before I could get out the car an old school box Chevy pulled up and two hooded niggas jumped out. They walked right towards Duke with their guns drawn. He was so busy entertaining those hoes he wasn't even paying attention to his surroundings. One butted him in the back of the head with the gun and he fell to the ground. The girls started screaming and running as they dragged that nigga and threw him in the backseat. They peeled off so fast they left tire tracks on the ground. I always kept my tool with me, but I couldn't get my burner hot for him. Plus, I'm in unfamiliar territory so I don't know who the opps are. I do know one thing though, Manny said he was a part of his team so this shit ain't looking good. I knew that lil nigga was nervous about something that day I met him. He probably scared shitless and he gonna sing like a canary. They should've just offed the nigga because a scared man ain't safe for me or Manny.

8

AMARI

"Dadddyyyyy!!!" CJ screamed as he ran to the door and embraced his father.

"Hey Jr. Have you gotten taller that quick? I only been gone for two months. Carver said as he hugged CJ. "What's up babymama?"

"Here you go with that babymama stuff again. I guess you found you a new bitch huh?" Carver had just arrived from Iowa, his new place of residence since we broke up.

"Don't start Amari, especially not in front of him." He was right because CJ was looking back and forth between us. "Daddy why mama mad at you?" CJ asked sensing the obvious tension between us. At only 5 years old, he is wise beyond his little years. "You staying home this time?" He was throwing him questions quicker than he could answer, and I was tickled pink on the inside.

"Whoa, whoa, whoa Jr, one question at a time. As a matter of fact, go put on your coat. You can ask me whatever you want on our way to Safari Land."

"Yaaaayyyyy, we going to Safari land!" CJ screamed as he skipped off to his room. "Make sure you brush your teeth first and pick up all those toys you got all over that room. And don't forget to turn that damn playstation off this time."

"Okay ma."

As soon as CJ was out of sight I hauled off and slapped the shit out of Carver. He grabbed my hand, "What the fuck is your problem and what I tell you about cursing at my got damn son."

He was looking at me like I had lost my mind. Truth is I probably had. I had just learned over the phone that he got another woman and had been waiting patiently to confront him in person. "Let me go! I was fuming mad. "So, you found you a Mexican bitch huh? How could you be with her and we ain't even been broke up a good month yet. You been cheating all along you lying bastard." I was holding back tears because the last thing I wanted him to think is that I'm bitter over some bitch. Before he came in town, we were on the phone talking about him coming here for the holidays. We had spent every year together as a family and just because we were broken up I didn't want my son to miss out what he's known his whole life. After ending our conversation, he didn't hang up his phone and I stayed on the line and listened. He was making plans with some Hispanic chic telling her he wouldn't be gone long and he was only coming here to see his son, not me. I knew our relationship was coming to an end. I did everything but tell him it was over. But to hear him with another woman firsthand hurt like hell.

"Amari you don't want me anymore. What you think I'm supposed to do? Wait for you to figure out if I'm who want. You wasn't even giving me sex anymore."

"Fuck you! I said trying to attack him again. He grabbed me and held me so close to his chest I could hear his heart beat. His smell, his embrace, I missed him so much. I had always been physically attracted to him. He stands about 5"9 with fair skin. He used to wear braids but his low fade complemented his strong facial features. Carver was muscular with strong arms and a smile that would light up any room. Puts me in the mind of Idris Elba. Being in his embrace made all my angry feelings towards him fade away instantly. Truth is he was a good ass man. He just got caught up in some bullshit while he was hustling and had to go on the run. After months of him sitting around the house babysitting and playing video games, I started to fall out of love with him. He noticed it too because I had started treating him differently. Every little thing he did had started to get on my nerves and I didn't even want him touching me. I was disappointed in the fact that once he couldn't sell drugs on the streets of Chicago, a nine to five didn't even cross his mind. Although he started off with big money, I had become the sole provider and he became content with it. That's the part that turned me off. I'll hold my nigga down if he falls off as long as he doesn't become content with his downfall. "I love you Carver." I could no longer hold back the tears because I sincerely love him. "You are a good man and an even better man to our son. You just couldn't provide for us anymore. I'm working 10 hour shifts and borrowing money from my mama to cover bills, buy food, and provide for CJ. I just couldn't get by off love anymore."

"You think I don't know that? You think I liked watching you come in at night complaining about your back and feet hurting you? You think I liked your mom coming around looking at me like I'm less than a man? That's why I had to leave Chicago. I had to make shit happen. Plus, ain't nothing in this city for me no more."

"We're here, your family." Tears were welling up in my eyes again. Dealing with my family no longer being together was killing me softly on the inside.

"Stop crying." Carver said wiping the tears from my face.

He went into his pocket and pulled out a huge stack of money and placed it in my hands. "What's this?" I don't know what the fuck he done went out of town and got into, but this is a lot of fucking money. More money than I've ever held in my hand at one time.

"It's what I've been doing since I've been gone out of town."

"So that means you're here to stay now right." I said getting excited at the idea of our family being back together. Plus, I was getting lonely as fuck. After being in a relationship for over seven years, being single, takes some getting used to.

"I can't stay. It's more money to be made." Carver said as he reached into his pocket and pulled out a blunt. "Let's go smoke."

Before going to smoke, I peeped in CJ's room to check on him. He was curled up in his bed with his hat and coat on, toys everywhere, the playstation on and stank breath. He ain't did nothing I said. I'm gone beat his lil ass when he get up. He think he slick, he only pulled that because his lil big head ass daddy here. "This is enough money for us to make it without you having to go back out of town. Plus, the income I got coming in from work. We can get a building or a store-front or something." I said following him to the garage, our desig-nated smoking area.

"That ain't enough to do shit. I have to go back, things are going too good right now."

"I found you a job too since I knew you'd be in town this week." That Mexican bitch ain't getting my babydaddy that easily. I hurried up and started doing job applications for him after I heard him tell that bitch he wouldn't be here long. I knew his social security number like it was mine and everything else about his identity, so it was easy to do the online applications.

"A job?" He asked looking at me like I'd just cursed him out. "A job where?"

"At the post office. All you got to do is show up for the test Monday at...

"Man I'm not finna go to no damn post office interview." He said interrupting me. They don't make shit there."

"They make enough for you to provide for your family and pay bills around here. I was getting angry all over again.

"Look you can save that job shit and that talk about buildings and storefronts. Have you forgot these niggas in Chicago got a price on my head? Do you know how long it will take to make that kind of money I just gave you at the post office? Shit you can even quit your job now."

"That's a temporary source of income. That's the same reason it's a price on your head now. When are you gonna realize that the drug game only leads to two things? At least the post office is a legit job and it will bring your family back together. I'm tired of CJ always asking me when you coming back home."

"See that's the main problem right there. You love me, but you been fell out of love with me. All you keep saying is how CJ wants his family together, that's all you care about."

"I can fall in love with you again, I will even move out of town with you."

"Oh, now you want to move? Why you didn't go with me when I first asked you?"

He did ask me to move out of town with him because he didn't want to be away from us. But I was scared to give up my stability. I been on my job for a year and had just got promoted to a supervisor. He said we were gonna stay with his brother until I found a job and he was able to get back on his feet. Apparently, he got back on his feet quicker than I anticipated. "Neither one of us had nothing and I wasn't about give up my life to go depend on your brother. But since you're settled in your own place now, we can come."

He stood up and passed me the blunt. "It's too late for that Amari."

"No, it's not, I can put in my two week notice and my...."

"She pregnant." He stopped me midsentence.

The whole garage started to spin. "She what? You got that Mexican whore pregnant!" I got up and started attacking him again. I couldn't believe it. He grabbed me firmly and looked me directly in my eyes.

"I'm sorry babymama." I cringed at that word. I had never been labeled a babymama because we had always been a couple. I was always bae, and in my mind, I was his wife. So, I despised that word. "You know I'm still gonna be a good father to CJ and I'm still gonna look out for you. I'm making major moves now and I will never forget about the person who held me down when I had nothing." Carver said as he walked towards the garage door. "I'm going to wake Jr up so we can head out. See you later."

I stayed in the garage and broke down crying. I waited for him and CJ to leave before going back into the house. I didn't want my baby to see me crying like this. Once again, the reality of my family being split hit me like a ton of bricks. After gathering my composure, I took a shower and put on my pink and silver Adidas jogging suit with the matching adidas shoes and headed to the bank.

"Would you like a balance receipt?" The teller asked.

"Yes please." I was still shocked at the news Carver had just sprang on me. He was about to have another baby. We had tried to have another baby, but I was never able to get pregnant again. If he got someone pregnant that soon, the problem must be me. That hurt me more than us not being together anymore.

"Enter your pin number please." The teller asked. "Ma'am." She said raising her voice a notch higher and breaking my daze.

"I'm sorry. I had a rough morning."

She flashed a fake smile as I entered my pin into the keypad. "Thank you for banking with Bank of America." She said while sliding the receipt across the counter.

"What you doing with that kind of money?"

"Oh my gosh, you again! Are you stalking me?" I said annoyed at the fact that Tray just happened to be the next customer in line and was apparently all in my business. I came to deposit that money Carver had just given me. I didn't want that kind of cash just sitting around the house. I didn't even count it, I didn't know how much it was until the teller gave me the transaction receipt. It was exactly $48, 000. I don't know what the hell he was into, but I definitely needed the money.

"Don't be like that." He said stepping out the line to follow me. "We got a lot in common. We club at the same club, bank at the same bank." He smiled and flashed those infectious dimples.

"You just don't give up do you?"

"Not when I see something I want, and it's been a long time since I saw anything worth my effort."

I mustered up my most sarcastic and irritated tone. "I'm flattered, but just like I told you before, I'm not interested." I hit the alarm on my 2016 Nissan Murano and reached for the door.

Tray beat me to the punch and opened the door for me. "Just take my number."

"My phone is dead." I said making up a quick lie. Although he is sexy, and his persistence is kinda cute, I needed time to get closure from my recent break up and right now I can't even entertain another man.

Tray reached inside his pocket and pulled out a business card. "Take this and use my cell number whenever you desire."

"Thank you." I flashed a fake smile and threw the card in my glove compartment. I just wasn't in the mood.

"So, you just gonna throw my card in the glove compartment huh? You're something else. But I promise you once you give me a chance you'll forget all about that lil baby daddy of yours." Tray said before walking back towards the bank. I'm starting to think this dude really stalking me. How the fuck he know I got a babydaddy.

9
___

TRAY

In other news, authorities say the male victim found in Bricksquare Projects located on Chicago's west side has been identified as Jeron Dickerson. A local resident discovered his body and contacted police officials. Reports say the victim suffered from one gunshot wound to the head. His body was there for weeks before being found. So far police have no lead on the victim's killer and no witnesses have come forward.

"Stop." I said to my housekeeper Maricella who was taking pleasure in giving me some early morning head. I hired her when I first moved out here to Floosmoor. I'd gotten me a mansion built from the ground up. I knew I wouldn't be able to keep up the homes needs, so I hired a live-in housekeeper. She was an immigrant from Cuba who was willing to work hard. She cleaned, cooked my favorite Cuban dishes, did my laundry, and did all the necessary shopping for the house. She even got her brother to upkeep the grass. The job included free rent, a car and a weekly paycheck. The fact that we fucked every now and then was an added bonus. Although I was enjoying it, the news reporter had gotten my attention.

"No Papi. You taste so gud." She replied as she tried to continue. My dick had went soft though. I stopped her and sat up to get the remote and adjust the volume on my 72-inch smart tv. She said something in Spanish and strutted out of the room in her sexy negligee maid uniform. She had dozens of them, so she always looked sexy while prancing around the house.

I didn't order no hit on JD and Manny knew better than to do some dumb shit like that in the hood. That type of shit only made the square hot and the last thing I need is homicide shutting down my operations for a murder investigation. This nigga was starting to feel himself. Don't nobody make moves like that on my territory without my order. Niggas coming up short on my money, work moving slower than ever all of a sudden, and now this.

"HEY TRAY, I haven't seen you around here in a while." Tracy said walking up to my car grinning from ear to ear proudly flashing her toothless smile.

I hopped in my Tesla and drove straight to the square after I watched the news. I didn't even shower because shit was weighing too heavy on my mind. "What's up lady." She was one of the neighborhood crackheads. I fucked with her because she is Chuck's little sister. Even though she smokes crack, I still treat her with love and respect. Back in the day she was one of the baddest females from over here. Then she got that monkey on her back and went from being the baddest to just looking bad.

"Man, these police hot as hell over here since they found that boy body. That's fucked up what happened to him but I'm trying to get my shit." She said while snorting and scratching her neck. "When they gone start back serving? That new shit yall put out is like butta and I need some more of that shit."

"Stick around, they'll be gone quicker than you can blink your eye. It's another dead black man in the projects. They don't give a fuck in real life." I was taking in the fact that she just said something about "new shit." I ain't gave Manny no new product in a while and I still got plenty from my last shipment. Tracy must be tripping. "So, you like that new shit huh?" I asked making sure I'd heard her right.

"Yea. Ever since they put it out a few weeks ago, everybody been talking about how good it is and the lines been longer than ever. Muthafuckas coming from all over Chicago for this new shit. But I ain't waiting in no lines. Them lil niggas know who I am. When I walk the fuck up they better serve me." Tracy said still living off the days her brother ran the hood. She still walked around like she was invincible. Even as a crackhead she had this larger than life attitude.

"Aight well bring that rich white nigga you be tricking off with through to spend some of that cash." I said dismissing the idea that she was tweaking. A fiend knows their drug and Tracy is a loyal customer. So, if she says it's some new shit moving, it's some new shit moving.

She pointed to a red 2 door Benz, "I'm already with him and I already got the cash." She looked towards the crack building and got excited when she noticed the last police car leave. "About time. I'll holla at you later Tray. I'mma go sit in the car with him until they start back serving. I just wanted to come say hi."

"Aight Tracy, it was good seeing you. Oh yea, who live in apartment 906 in that building?" Niggas will threaten other niggas to silence but these crackheads be knowing more about what's going on than these goofy ass young dudes and will run anything down for a $10 high.

"906...906." She repeated trying to jog her own memory. "Oh yea, that's my homegirl apartment. Well it used to be hers, she left it with her two daughters, Monique and Kyra." Tracy remembered.

"Aight Trac, stay out of trouble." I had Tracy to slide me a bag of that new shit. Soon as she put it in my hands I knew it wasn't my work. But the shit bagged up in my bags and being sold on my fucking territory. Somebody is ready to die. Before I pulled off I put in a call to Tezza. *Hey Tezza. I need another favor.* She is the office manager at the housing authority. We used to mess around years back when I was still sweating packs. She left me for a nigga who was older than me and had more paper. I bet she regret that shit now. She got pregnant by him and they got married. He fell off a few years later and now he's a janitor working under her. I paid her under the table from time to time to get what I needed done with certain apartments.

"*Hey Tramaine Wallace.*" She said stating my whole government name.

"*What I tell you about saying my name like that over the phone?*" Although I used untraceable throw away phones, you could never be too careful.

"*Whatever, what apartment and what you need done?*" She was always irritated when I called.

She was still salty because she be shooting her shot and I pass every time. I really used to be digging on her when I was a shorty and she crushed my young heart when she left me for that lame ass nigga. "*906, eviction. Make up something and make it good. I want them out immediately.*" I could've easily gotten them killed but I was trained under a real G. So, I stuck to the old g-code, women and kids are off limits. I never killed or ordered hits on women, but it was more than one way to skin a cat. These young niggas out here killing anything moving, pregnant women, old people and babies with no remorse. That's why I was ready to get out the game. Shit was just different now. These lil niggas don't honor and respect the g code no more.

"You still ain't ready to talk?" I said to Duke as I puffed on my Cuban cigar. He'd been in the basement of one of my peoples house, well torture chamber. I had Choppa and Fendi to kidnap him a few weeks ago and he had been down here tied to the chair ever since. He had pissed and shitted on himself and looked like he was dying of thirst and hunger. He a lil chunky mutherfucker too so I know he ain't used to missing meals. Manny had him running 2103, the crack building. When word got out that he was riding around in a new car, a 2018 Audi with 22s and sounds, I knew he was part of the reason my work was moving slow and my money was coming up short. But I kept him alive because a dead man couldn't give me the information I needed. He was slightly unconscious as he sat in the chair bleeding from his mouth. "Whose shit is this?" I threw the bag of crack I'd gotten from Tracy in his face.

"I swear I don't know Tray."

"Take off his pinky fingers." He squealed in pain as Choppa cut off his left pinky finger with a pair of lock cutters. He got a thrill from doing torturous shit. He didn't use guns, he liked using chainsaws and shit. Manny was the trigger happy one. So, I went to Choppa when I wanted a mufucka tortured. He would chop a dude head off with a smile on his face, that's how he got the nickname Choppa. Right as he was going for Dukes right pinky he started pleading for his life.

"Okay, please don't kill me. I swear I had no choice. Manny threatened to kill my whole family if I didn't go along with his plan. That's his work. I swear it's not mines. He working with some dude from out of town named Romell. Please don't kill me."

"Manny as in my Manny?" I dropped my cigar and stomped it out then walked closer to Duke. "So instead of coming to me about it, you decided to go along with that nigga?"

"I didn't know how to get in touch with you and you ain't been to the hood in a minute. I told Manny I wanted out, but he came to my house and threatened to kill my grandma, my kids, and their mother. I did it to protect them. I wouldn't lie to you Tray."

Duke had a lot of heart because Choppa been torturing him for the last few weeks and he just breaking. A coward nigga would've told as soon as they kidnapped him. I knew he was telling the truth though. Manny was a heartless ass nigga. He used to be my right-hand but I distanced myself from him when I noticed how the money and status was changing him. That's the difference between me and him, I didn't let my rank or money change me because you can be here today and gone tomorrow and I don't take shit for granted, especially in this drug game. But I still kept that nigga on my team because he didn't show me nothing but loyalty. "You got a lot of heart Duke and I know what it's like to want to protect your family. But you fucked up when you start spending my money on cars and rims instead of coming to me. Now how a dead man gonna protect his family?" I pulled out my .38 and shot him execution style. I removed the handkerchief from my pocket to dab the blood splatter from my face. "Clean this up and get rid of his body." I instructed Choppa and Fendi.

Duke confirmed what I already knew. I just didn't think that nigga had the balls to double cross me. I taught him everything he knows, and people only feared and respected him because they feared and respected me. I haven't been in the streets heavy over the pass years because I'm getting up in age. And lately I've been more focused on my business ventures than the dope game. So, all I do is give orders and Manny pretty much filling my shoes. I guess he thinks I ain't focused on what's going on, but I count all my dollars and pay attention to everything. Manny forgot I used to be a young hothead who would kill a nigga just for coming up short on a pack. I just closed a few business deals that would allow me to retire from the game for good. I didn't want to wind up like Chuck, not being able to enjoy my riches and only passing the torch because I was finna spend the rest of my days in prison. But I gotta remind these young niggas of who the fuck I am.

10

MONIQUE

If it wasn't for bad luck I guess I wouldn't have none. I come to our apartment only to find a fucking eviction notice on the door. I called the housing office and that dirty bitch Tezza gone say I got unauthorized guests living in my unit and that's a violation of the lease. There was no way to avoid eviction. Kyra was missing in action and her phone wasn't on because she hasn't paid her bill. If I don't pay it, it won't get paid and I'm tired of that shit. She almost grown. But I still wanna know where the fuck she at and why she ain't have the decency to at least call me to tell me we getting put the fuck out. I haven't heard from Ro ever since I left him sitting on my couch. I was still mad and wanted to make him know it, so I played hard to get thinking he would learn his lesson. But that made shit worse because he has made no effort to contact me. Aside from the fact that he was beating on me like I was his personal punching bag, he had good ways about himself. He was a gangsta and a gentleman. And he's done more for me over these pass couple months than anybody has ever done for me my whole life. I had developed feelings for him and I low key missed his crazy ass. I'm tired of ripping and running these streets turning tricks. I just wanna be a kept bitch by a paid nigga. Since I had no contact number on him I drove out to his

Condo in Hickory Hills to pop up on his ass, low and behold it was a for rent sign in the window. "What the fuck." On top of everything else, I was low on cash and my car note was due. I didn't even know I had a fucking car note until I got a letter in the mail from the finance company saying my car was up for repossession. I only had it for three months so that means this nigga just put a down payment on a car and never paid the note. I need a few thousand asap or I'm about to be homeless and back on the bus.

"Hey Manny," I put in a call to him because he was always ready to trick some cash. I tricked off with him for the first time when I was 15 years old. Me and my sister were in the house by ourselves starving to death. He spotted me at the corner store begging the Arab man for a pack of hotdogs and a loaf of bread. Needless to say, the bastard turned me down. As many food stamps as me and my mother had spent in that lil raggedy ass store, you would think he would've given em to me. I was crying and everything because the hunger pains were so intense. Manny was at the counter buying blunts and saw every-thing. He followed me out the store and told me to go with him and he would buy me and my sister something to eat. He took me up the street to McDonalds and told me to order anything I wanted. On the way back to drop me off he went in his pocket and gave me a $100. I was happy as hell. That all went away when he pulled in the back of the parking lot and told me nothing in life is free and I would have to earn that money. I wanted to get out that car so bad, but I didn't know where we would get our next meal from so I stuck around. He took my virginity right in the car and taught me how to suck dick. Seeing how he was a full-grown man at the time, it had hurt like hell. But doing it to him in my adult years, I barely felt it. He was 5 inches at his hardest.

"*Hey money Monique.*" I hated when he called me that shit. He found humor in the fact that I used what he taught me and ran with it. A nigga couldn't hold a five-minute conversation with me without giving me some money.

"*What's up friend. I need a favor. I'm strapped for cash and I need a few thousand.*"

"You know what you gotta do."

"Yea I know. What time can we meet. I need the money like yesterday."

"I'm gonna get a Jacuzzi suite at the Champagne lodge out in the suburbs. I'll send you the address when I'm ready."

∼

"S<small>EE</small> you always gotta do some extra shit. What she doing here?" He shot me a text and I met him at the room. He was already sitting there with some chick drinking.

"You said you wanted to make some extra money right? Well she do too. So, I figured we can all make some money together." He said as he flashed a big wad of 100 dollar bills with a slick smirk on his face. I came across a lil extra cash and I'm feeling friendly. But yall gotta cooperate."

Now what the fuck he finna do with two women and that lil ass dick I thought to myself. "This wasn't part of the deal, so you better be paying extra nigga." I wasn't really into women sexually, but he'd been asking me about a threesome for a long time now and I kept turning him down. But I need money so any extra money I could get, I need. That's why he picked now to pull this threesome shit. He knows I need the money. I'm beating myself up now that I think about how much money I was blowing since I'd met Ro. I should've been stacking that cash instead of trying to keep up with the Jones. I just thought he would be around longer and that money would be there. Boy was I wrong.

He slapped my butt with the cash he was holding, "Didn't I just tell you I'm feeling friendly." He reached in his pocket and passed me a pill. "Here, pop this, me and her already started." I swallowed the pill and followed it with a shot of patron before walking into the bathroom to freshen up. By the time I came out, they were already in the Jacuzzi.

"Hey Monique."

I'm wondering why she speaking to me like she know me, but when I got closer I recognized her face. "Hey Tangie." She was another girl from the hood who was always tricking these niggas for cash. She was a nice looking female. Her shoulder length blunt cut was on point and she had curves for days. With D cups, a small waist, and a big butt, it was easy for her to attract ballers. Shit looking at her naked body in this Jacuzzi, I'm suddenly attracted.

Manny broke me out my thoughts. "Come on ladies, let's toast to a good freaky night." He said holding up his champagne glass. "Yall thick as fuck. I'm about to have a great fucking night."

He turned to the porn channel as we were finishing our last cup. By now I was completely intoxicated and ready for whatever. I felt the sexual energy coming from Tangie and it turned me on. I watched the water glisten off her skin. It was the sexiest thing seeing another woman naked. Manny pulled me against his hardening penis and began fingering my clit. Tangie joined him and started swirling her tongue around my nipples. A tingly sensation shot through my whole body. I took her breast in my mouth and flickered my tongue around her nipple. The foreplay had my pussy throbbing hard as hell. The pleasure became too intense for the water, so we made our way to the king-size bed. I lay back on the bed as I enjoyed oral sex from a woman for the first time. Her warm mouth and amazing tongue skills had my juices flowing. Manny was taking Tangie from behind. "Yes, eat that pussy baby and take daddy dick." Switching positions, I climbed on top of Manny to ride him while Tangie sat on his face. He nutted four minutes into me riding him. I knew that was gonna happen. He took off the lifestyle condom, dropped it in the trash, and walked towards the bathroom.

"That's it." Tangie said clearly still sexually frustrated.

I laughed because she's obviously never had sex with him. Manny's cell phone vibrating on the nightstand distracted me. I looked at the caller ID. It was an incoming call from Romell. "What the hell." I said aloud to myself. How the hell does he know Romell.

"What?" Tangie asked breaking my thoughts.

"Nothing." I got out the bed and eased his phone off the table. I opened up the call log and noticed several missed calls from Romell. I went to the text messages because curiosity was getting the best of me. It was a slew of messages between the two of them. I looked towards the bathroom to make sure Manny wasn't coming out. "Let me know when he come out the bathroom." I strolled through the messages and was shocked at the content of them. Not only did these niggas plot on me, they plotting on Tray? You would think with the content of their conversation this nigga would have erased his messages. I walked towards the stand with the hotel phone on it and grabbed the pen and pad. I quickly wrote down Tray's number.

"Here he come." Tangie whispered loudly.

"Shit." I didn't get a chance to write Romell's number down, so I tried to mentally record it before putting his phone back where I got it. He walked right towards it and picked it up and started strolling through it.

"We gotta check out early." Manny said as he started getting dressed. "I gotta go."

"I'm kind of drunk and I don't want to drive so I'm gonna check out in the morning."

He nodded his head and said okay before going into his pockets. He counted out $5000 for both me and Tangie. "I'll holla at yall later."

"Did you enjoy your first threesome?" Tangie asked once he was out of the room. She was still in the bed naked waiting to get an orgasm.

"It was okay. A bigger dick would've helped."

She busted out laughing. "You said that. And he swears he was doing something. *Take daddy's dick.*" She said imitating him." She grabbed her Louis V bag and placed the money he'd just given her in and pulled out a silver bullet. "But how did you enjoy being with a woman?"

"I liked it more than I thought I would."

"Well let me finish what he started then. Lay back." She turned the silver bullet on and placed it on my clitoris. I was no longer in the mood for sex, so I wasn't into it. My mind was working a mile a minute as I registered what I'd just read in his phone. Manny ain't been doing nothing but taking advantage of me since I was a lil girl.

Romell used me, played with my feelings and kicked me to the curb. Well karma is a bitch because they fucked over the right one. I was about to use this newfound information to my monetary advantage. I found out more than I needed to know, enough information to get them both killed. I was definitely about to use this information wisely.

$\sim$

"HEY TRAYYY." I sang into the phone in my most sexy voice. Tangie caught an Uber home and I was at the front desk turning in the room keys and checking out.

"Who is this?"

"Monique. You do remember me, right?"

"How did you get my number and what do you want?" He was being rude as hell and I wanted to say fuck it and hang up, but I got motives, so I dismissed his attitude.

"I got some valuable information I think you can use. Can we meet in person?"

11

MANNY

Romell been blowing my line up. I wanted to lay low for a while until the buzz of JD's murder died down. I took the 32k I got from him and decided to blow it on some clothes and hoes. So, it was nothing for me to give those hoes that $10,000. That's how shit was finna be from now on. Once I take over this city Imma have all these hoes at my beck and call. Bitches used to play me when was I was broke and dirty but they gonna regret that shit. Ro was my cellie when I was serving time in East Moline for a gun case I had caught a few years back. He was a cool nigga with roots in Iowa. He was finishing up a bid for being caught crossing state lines with a few kilos. I gained his loyalty when he got into a fight on the yard with some young niggas from Chicago. I helped him whoop the shorties with no questions asked. We became close for the rest of the time and held each other down. If I had commissary and he didn't I looked out for him and vice versa. We even got a lil money together in prison selling cell phones to other inmates. He said his people got fronted some kilos and he was gonna be making major moves when he got out. Although he had gotten out before me, he stayed true to his word. Let me see what this nigga want. *"What's up Ro? You been blowing a nigga phone up. I got your text, what's so urgent?"*

"Man where the fuck you been?" Have you heard from Duke?"

"Naw I haven't heard from him. But I know where he at. He should be through with that work so I'mma hit him up to pick up the money."

"That's why I been trying to reach yo ass nigga. Duke got kidnapped a few weeks ago by two dudes in a white box Chevy. What the fuck is going on?"

"What you mean he got kidnapped? Where this happen?"

"Nigga in your hood. The same hood you told me you had shit on lock at. He was in the parking lot in a new Audi with sounds bumping loud as hell talking to some hoes and then two niggas ran up on him, knocked him out, and put him in the car in less than 60 seconds."

"A new Audi? I told that mufucka don't start spending money like that. Shit attracts too much attention. That's probably some niggas trying to rob him. Let me see what I can find out and Imma hit you back." Fuck! If Duke got kidnapped that means Tray on to what we doing. If he still alive he betta keep it G and take one for the team. If he dead and went out like a bitch, they about to have a family funeral. I couldn't let Romell on to the fact that I wasn't really running shit like I had told him when we was locked up. Niggas lie everyday in jail. I never thought for a minute that nigga would come through with all that work.

"Yea aight. Hit me back asap because we gotta pay these people back and they want their money."

I don't know why he speaking French because we ain't gotta pay back shit. He gotta pay them mufuckas back. "I got you." I said before ending the call. Look like I got to put a plan b in motion because the last thing I need is him and Tray coming at my neck about my money. I tried to hit Duke line, but it kept going straight to voicemail. I hopped in my BMW and took lake shore drive to head to Duke grandmother's house. I was hungry and had a taste for some breakfast food so, I put in an order at one of my favorite spots in hyde park, Mellow Yellow. Traffic was heavy as fuck and I was getting impatient. I took a shot of the Remy I had in my passenger seat while waiting for the slow ass traffic to move. I turned the Bluetooth on my phone and 21 Savage came rapping through the car stereo, "I got 1, 2, 3, 4, 5, 6, 7, 8,

M's in my bank account." I adjusted the volume because that song was the motivation. *"I got 1, 2, 3, 4, 5, 6, 7, 8 shootas ready to gun ya down... ready to gun ya down."* I will soon have 8 mill and some in my bank account I thought as I bumped to the music and took another shot. And any mutherfucka that get in the way of that will be gunned down.

Traffic finally picked up and I exited at 47th to pick up my food. After I finished my hash browns and steak omelet, I stopped by Duke's grandmother crib. "Hey Mrs. Reed." I greeted her after Duke's babymama, Crystal, finally opened the door. She was laying on the living room sofa hooked up to an oxygen tank. Although she was sickly and could no longer get around, her mind was as sharp as a pencil and she hated my guts. She blamed me for Duke getting in the drug game, but that shit ain't my fault. He was out here robbing niggas and selling drugs way before I came home.

"What you doing over here and where the hell is my grandson?" She snatched the oxygen mask off as soon as she locked eyes with me and I could see fire coming from them. "I haven't seen my baby in over three weeks and I know you got something to do with it." She could barely breathe as she tried getting off the couch like she was about to attack me. "I know something is wrong. I just feel it."

Crystal ran to her aide because she almost fell over and was gasping for air at this point. "Calm down grandma Reed. Duke gonna be ok." She lay her back down and put the oxygen mask on her face.

"I haven't heard from him Mrs. Reed. That's why I'm here. I was hoping one of yall had." She gave me another evil blank stare as a single tear rolled down her cheek.

Crystal walked towards the kitchen and motioned for me to follow her. "I'll be there in a minute." I didn't come here for them to harass me about Duke´s whereabouts. I went downstairs to the base-ment where Duke kept the stash. The smell of sewer mixed with moth balls hit my nose soon as I touched the bottom step of the unfinished basement. I walked around the large puddle of water that was backing out of the drain to make it the half bathroom. I peeled off the four square tiles under the shower head to access the stash. I loaded my empty bag with everything in there, including some of Tray's work. I left out without seeing what Crystal wanted. I don't know what she wanted me to tell her. I hit the trunk button on my key and loaded the bag of dope and money before peeling off.

Aside from the money I'd been stacking from working for Tray, I'd robbed him a few times as well. JD was another nigga that fell victim to my plot. Truth is he never came up short on the 50k. I linked up with my cousin who is a Chicago police officer and included him on my plan. I offered him his years salary times two if he staged a few hits on the building. I made sure he came right when the buildings was reloaded. My cousin was an OG who used to rob niggas for a living. He got the opportunity to walk the straight and narrow when he was offered a job as a police officer. He jumped at the chance to leave the street life because he had watched all his childhood friends get killed or incarcerated. But even though he wore that badge of honor, deep down inside he was a cold-hearted criminal. He involved one his fellow officers and they had pulled off four hits so far. I now had enough money to cut out the middle man and go straight to the plug. I just gotta figure out how to get to Tray before that nigga get to me. Now that he found out about my plot it's time for me to soldier up. I'm kinda glad he found out now because there can only be one nigga running this city anyway.

12

AMARI

The turmoil of Carver having another woman pregnant had gotten the best of me. Turns out Carver had brought her to Chicago with him and had her tucked at some hotel. Guess she was feeling insecure about him coming around me and decided to tag along. I decided to let CJ leave town with his father for Christmas break because I just didn't want him to see me like this. He came to pick CJ up and brought her in to meet me. I needed to see the woman who would be spending time around my child anyway, so I didn't trip. Although I refused to let that bitch see it, my whole body went numb as I watched her and her pregnant belly walk out the door with my family. I been calling off work for the last few days just sitting around the house drinking and smoking trying to take in the events of my life. Ideally, I'm supposed to be married to a hardworking man raising our family and living our happily ever after. Yet here I am sitting on the edge of my bed watching my drunken reflection stare back at me. I had been crying and drinking so much I was starting to get bags under my eyes. But I brought this on myself. Carver was a good man and I fucked around and lost him to a Mexican bitch. I became impatient too soon because I knew he wasn't the type of guy that would be broke for long. He used to tell me he had nightmares of being broke so he hustled relentlessly. He got into something out there in those streets last year that brought that hustle to a screeching halt. To this day he's never told me what happened just that it was a matter of life or death. I knew it was serious because he was seeing too much money to just stop all of a sudden. We lived off what he'd saved up then eventually I had to find a job. He was stressed about not being able to make money and it brought stress on the relationship. We had started to argue over the pettiest things because we were spending too much time around each other. He stopped getting his hair cut and just sat around smoking weed, playing video games with CJ and being paranoid. That's when I drifted away.

But before then, I didn't want for shit. We met when I was a junior in high school and he was a local drop out. I would always stand on the same bus stop to get home and every day after school he would stop by in his ol'skool Monte Carlo with the spinners and basically stalk me. I finally gave in one day and I haven't seen a bus stop since. He took his lil pack money and bought me my first car, a little red 4 door Chevy Corsica. I smiled at that memory because I was happy as hell and bragged to all my friends about it at school the next day. He took me on my senior prom the following year, I gave up my virginity, and we had been together ever since. My cell phone rang breaking me from my thoughts. I reached over to the nightstand and pulled the charger out of my cell phone and looked at the caller id. It was Monique. *"Hello."*

"Hey friend, wake up. I need you." She was crying in the phone and that surprised me because she didn't cry often.

"I'm woke, what's wrong?"

"Everything! Where do I start? Shit is all bad." She let out a few sobs and I could hear her sniffling through the phone. I got an instant headache because I just stopped my own tears from flowing and here she go with her problems. *"We got put out and have nowhere to go."*

"Put out for what? Bitch I know you been paying your rent." She had my full attention now.

"*What rent Mari? I don't pay rent for that damn apartment, it's low income.*"

"*Did you call the housing authority?*"

"*Yea, that dirty slut Tezza been doing crooked shit in that office for years. She gone tell me I got unauthorized guests living with me. She got proof of Romell coming and going with a key like he lived there.*"

"*Damn that's fucked up. So where is your little sister?*"

"*That's another thing that's messing me up. I haven't heard from her in weeks and her cell phone is off. I'm worried sick about her. You know how drunk she be, anything could have happened to her.*"

"*Have you talked to any of her friends?*"

"*She don't have friends, but the ones that I have ran into haven't seen or heard from her either. I even went to the liquor store she frequents, and she hasn't been there. I don't know what to do. It feels like my whole world has been falling apart. Can I please come stay with you until I figure out what I'm gonna do.*"

I love my friend to death, but we lived totally different lifestyles now. We were inseparable as kids up until high school. I met Carver and was no longer hanging out with her, I remember her telling me I been acting funny ever since I met him. It wasn't that, I was just growing up and wanted more out of life. She had started ditching class and running the streets and we just grew apart. I chose to work and go to school, she chose to drop out and sell her body. I never judged her for what she did or looked at her any different. In my eyes, she's just the female version of a hustler. But I didn't want her lifestyle nowhere around my son. "*Wow, we got to talk about that one. I don't want none of that shit you be doing around my son.*"

"*What shit I be doing? Girl we do the same shit.*" She said like I'd just hurt her feelings. *You smoke weed, party, and fuck niggas just like I do. The fuck?*"

Even in her time of need she couldn't resist the urge to get flip at the lip. That mouth of hers got her ass whooped all her life. Between her slick tongue and her fucking on people men, she was the reason for every fight I ever had growing up. "*Girl I go to work EVERYDAY.*" I said putting emphasis on it. *She got a lot of nerve.* "*I been with the same nigga for the past seven years and I don't party half as much as you do.*"

"*You right, I'm sorry.*" She said humbling herself. "*Can I come? I've been staying in hotels, but I'm strapped for cash.*"

"*CJ out of town with his father until after the New Year when school start back so you can sleep in his room until then. But you better figure life out friend, we're getting older and you need stability in your life.*" She let out a deep breath as if I was irritating her, but I could care less. Every chance I got I tried talking some sense into her. She needed to hear it from somebody.

"*Okay, okay. I get it. When I finish getting my stuff put in storage, I'll call to make sure you're home. Thanks friend, you're always here for me.*"

That phone call had just blew me, so I went to my stash to roll up another blunt. I was out of swishers, so I got dressed to go to the gas station for more. I sat in my car and remembered I had a few packs of diamond swishers in the glove department. Reaching inside, I noticed Tray's business card. Since Carver had moved on it was about time I did the same. I grabbed his card and shot him a text message:

Me: Hey, I finally decided to use your number.

Tray: I'm glad you did, now when you gonna let me take you out?

Me: You don't even know who this is.

Tray: Of course I do, how could I forget you.

Me: LOL. Is that right?

Tray: I been waiting on you to hit me up, but I don't really do the texting thing so call me cutie.

AFTER A MUCH NEEDED NAP, I got up to get ready for my date. I agreed to go out with Tray and I was already running late. I quickly got up to get dressed. I changed clothes at least five times before deciding what to wear. I hadn't been on a date in a long time and I wanted to look good. I chose my black rock jeans and a black sheer long sleeved blouse that stopped right about my navel. I wanted to let a lil skin show but not too much. I adorned my jeans with a

Gucci belt to match my knee length Gucci stiletto boots. After freshening up my hair and doing my make up, he was already outside. I grabbed my red coat with the bell bottom sleeves and Gucci purse out the closet and hurried up and dumped the contents of my other purse on my bed so I could switch. I dabbed on my favorite scent and left out the door. "Hey Tray." I said as I climbed in the passenger seat of his Tesla admiring the custom interior. "This is very nice."

"Thanks. I picked out everything myself. You smell good enough to eat. What scent is that?" He asked as he backed out of my driveway.

"Chanel." I responded as I observed the expensive bracelet he was sporting. I also noticed that for the third time he was wearing a fancy business suit. "What you do for a living. Your business card says you're a pharmacist, but I don't know one pharmacist that drives a Tesla, got diamonds like that, and wears $5000 suits.

He laughed but I was so serious. "I'm a pharmacist baby, I just been doing it for over a decade now. And I know how to save and invest."

"Oh okay, so where we going?" I couldn't be out all night because I had to work in the morning and I had no more vacation time or sick days.

"Don't worry about it. You're with me, just sit back, kick your feet up and relax."

"I just wanted to know how late you think you're keeping me out because I got work in the morning."

He reached on the side of the door and pulled out a zip lock bag full of weed. "You smoke?"

"Yes."

"It just keeps getting better, where is your cell phone?" He passed me the weed and a pack of raw blunt raps.

"Right here." I said reaching in my purse to retrieve it. "Why?"

"Roll this up and call your job. Tell them you're not gonna be able to make it in the morning."

I was lost as to why he was telling me to call off from my job, but I called anyway. "I know I haven't been there all week, I told you my son was sick." I was explaining to my supervisor why I needed another day off when Tray snatched the phone from me.

"Hello Ms. Supevisor, how are doing?" He asked and then paused. She must've asked him who he was because his next statement threw me off. "I'm her man. You might want to get another person for that position because she won't be coming back to your slave ship." He said and pressed end before handing me back my phone.

"Now why would you do that? I can't be quitting my job, I got bills and a kid to take care of and who said I was your woman." This man was cockier than I could handle, and he had just lost his damn mind telling my supervisor that dumb shit. I hit redial to call her back.

He snatched the phone again and refused to give it back. "When you decided to use my number, you became my woman. And the only thing my woman gotta do with her time is donate to charity."

I was speechless. I didn't know what I was in store for with this man, but he definitely got my attention. I was tired of working anyway and was about to use the money Carver been giving me to fulfill my childhood dream of owning my own salon. "Well alrighty then." We cruised the city streets while we got more acquainted and smoked our brains out. He took me downtown to Fogo De Chao and I stuffed myself silly. I had never been there, and the experience was amazing. I ate that meat quicker than those men could march it out to our table. I had to ask him why they kept bringing me food and he told me to turn my stopper over to the red side. As long as the green side was showing they would keep bringing it out. I was embarrassed at my lack of fine dining. I thought red lobster was fine dining, but boy was I wrong. "I had a good time tonight. I'm glad I'm came out." We were back in his car and headed to my place to take me home. I moved on the north side a long time ago because it's one of the more safer neighborhoods in Chicago.

"You live far as hell." He said as we were driving west on I-94 approaching the divide between O'Hare airport and the north suburbs.

"Yea, I moved as far away from the projects as possible. I wanted to move somewhere where he can ride his bike outside peacefully on summer days and get the same education these white kids getting in the fall.

"I can't say I blame you for that." He said distractedly as he looked through his rearview and jumped out the lane over to the O'hare lane exits.

"You should've stayed over there, you can't get to my house this way." He blocked me out and pressed his gas pedal all the way to the floor. My heart started racing and I started to panic. I knew I shouldn't have got in the car with him. This nigga about to kidnap me. I started screaming when I saw him reach under his seat and pull a long shiny silver gun. He aimed it towards me and I closed my eyes and started to plead for my life. He let off seven shots right in the middle of the fucking highway and I just knew I was dead. But when the gunfire stopped, I looked up and breathed a sigh of relief because I was still in the land of the living. As he swerved in and out of lanes trying to get the fuck out of dodge, I turned around and looked out the back window. He had shot up a black BMW and caused a multi car collision. Police cars were coming out of nowhere. I just let this man quit my job for me and agreed to be his woman and he´s a fucking maniac. What the fuck have I gotten myself into.

I KNEW I should have told him no when he asked me to come in. After witnessing what I just saw, I should've got out his car, walked away and never looked back. Instead, I allowed him to come and make love to me all night. When he left the next morning, I needed someone to talk to, so I told Monique everything. Her advice was to leave him alone because I couldn't handle the lifestyle he lives. I lay in bed with mixed emotions. He was everything I wanted in a man and just what I needed to help me get over Carver. But it's evident that even though he's a gentleman on the outside, on the inside he's a cold hearted gangsta.

13

TRAY

It had been over a week and she was still ignoring my calls. I knew better than to make a move like that, but I blacked out and my anger got the best of me when I spotted Manny's car. That nigga had fell under the radar and nobody knew of his whereabouts. He was finna try to pull a ghost move and leave town and I couldn't let that happen. He been fucking up my money for a while and he gone pay my shit back with his blood. JD shot me a text that morning that he was meeting with that nigga and told me he was giving him 32k. So, when he hit my line and said JD didn't give him nothing I knew he was lying. This nigga done crossed me in every way possible and now he just a breathing skeleton.

I apologized to Amari because I didn't mean for her to see that side of me, especially not so soon. I was enjoying her company so much and I don't know when the last time I was that attracted to a woman. She is exactly who I need to sit beside me on my throne. She was already hard to get so I hope I didn't chase her away. But I'm gonna fall back until I take care of these niggas then I'm coming back for my queen.

"What took you so long to come to the door?" I went by Ivory's house to see my son and get some info from his mother.

"I was in the bathroom." She came to the door in her two-piece Victoria secret panty and bra set. She a lil horny ass nympho. She was always in the mood for sex whenever I came around.

"Why you half dressed? Where is my son?" I walked past her to make my way towards lil Tray room. Sex was the furthest thing from my mind.

"He went to movies with his friend. He'll be back in a few hours." She said stopping me in my tracks.

"Didn't I tell you I was on my way over here. Why the fuck you let him leave? I haven't seen my son in almost a month." Between my new business deals and that shit that's been going on at the square, I haven't been able to spend a lot of time with him lately. He is another reason I'm ready to leave the game. I wanna see my seed fully blossom and be around to keep a whip to his back. He will never live the life I've lived as long as I got breath in my body.

"Because he wanted to go." She said in a smart voice. "That lil boy been talking about that damn movie ever since he saw the preview and it came out today. I told you he'll be back in a few hours, damn. And I'm half dressed because I was hoping I could get some dick before he come back.

"I thought you said you could get dick elsewhere." I said reminding her of her smart-ass comment. "What happened? That nigga ain't fuck you right?"

"I don't want dick from nowhere else. I was just saying that to piss you off. I could get dick from anybody I want, but you ain't gonna do nothing but chase them away like you always do." She said and strutted off with an attitude.

"Naw them niggas just can't fuck you like I do."

"Naw, I just want MY dick." She said putting emphasis on the word. "I know you fucking that skank ass housekeeper bitch Maricella. She must've sucked your dick this morning before you came over here. That's why I'm whooping her ass the minute the bitch cross my path. Ol' homewrecking hoe. I can't wait for Trump to build that wall, so she can take her ass back to her country."

I had to laugh at her crazy ass. "Damn how long you been holding that in?" Ain't nobody fucking Maricella. Where the fuck you get that from?"

She walked into the living room to cut on her surround sound stereo. "Think I'm stupid if you want to. It ain't shit I don't know about you. I'm wifey nigga."

She played In My Mind by Heather Headley. She was dropping subliminal hints like a muthafucka through the song. I must admit she did look good as hell with her ass hanging out those thongs like that. I took off my suit jacket and put it on the coat hook in the foyer after getting a Cuban cigar from the pocket. I followed her into the living room, grabbed an ash tray off the fireplace mantle, and sat on the couch. "Ivory I got so much shit on my mind my dick probably won't even get hard."

"Damn, it's that bad? Tell me what's on your mind. Just know when you finish, I'm gone get that dick hard." She joked but was serious at the same time.

"Remember that nigga I had you to follow in the building that day? You said his name was Romell right?"

"Yea, why what's up?" By now I had diverted her mind from sex and she was focused on what I was saying. She picked up the remote and muted the radio.

"Did you get his number?"

"Yea."

"I need you to call him and find out his location. That nigga been moving work on my territory." I said as I took a long pull on my cigar. Hearing myself say that out loud was fueling the rage on the inside of me. I still can't believe niggas thought that shit was cool.

"How the fuck he been doing that? You got a lot of people in place to make sure shit like that don't happen."

"That snake ass nigga Manny set it up."

She bucked her eyes in surprise. "You fucking lying! Not your boy."

Ivory is the only person I've ever put an ounce of trust in. She's had a nigga back since day one and will go to the moon and back for me. I opened up to her more when I lost my mother three years ago.

My mom was crazy about her especially after she had given her her first grandchild. In her eyes Ivory could do no wrong and she pressured me on a regular to marry her. My mom used to be my best friend and confidante and that was what Ivory became to me after I lost her.

"Yea, my boy. I caught that nigga trying to leave town and emptied my clip in his car while he was speeding up the expressway. I don't know if he dead or not, but I got my people on it."

"Shit Tray. You don't supposed to be out there getting your hands dirty like that. You shooting outta cars on the expressway. What you trying to do get locked the fuck up? You got too much to lose. Where the fuck is your team?"

She was right about me getting my hands dirty and that's why I confided in her. She was the only person who let me know when I'm doing some fucked up shit. Everybody else be so intimidated by who I am that they just agree with whatever I say or do, a bunch of yes men. "Them niggas moving too fucking slow. They gotta wake up early in the morning to keep up with a snake ass nigga like him. And they obviously lacking because if I didn't happen to be driving on the highway that day he'd be fucking ghost."

"I feel you, but you still need to be careful out there. Them people been trying to get some dirt on you for years. It'll make their day to be able to handcuff and lock you up for anything."

"I can't argue with you when you right." I put the cigar out in the ashtray and asked her to go get me a bottle of water. The Chicago police know exactly who I am and have tried to take me down a few times to no avail. They could never catch me with my hands dirty because I was always one up on they ass.

She came back in the living room with the water and her cell phone in her hand. "You want me to call him now?"

"Yea, put it on speaker and call him up."

Beeeeeepppp......the mobile number you have dialed is no longer in service. If you feel you've reached this message in error, please hang up and dial again.....beep, beep..beep. "Damn, so what you gonna do now? You need me to do anything else?" She asked as she ended the call and sat her cell on the end table.

"Naw. I'll find that nigga. Don't worry about it."

She walked back to the radio and turned on T-Shirt and panties by Adina Howard. Here she go again I thought to myself, mind right back on sex. She climbed on top of me and buried my head in her chest. *"Body's hot, soaking wet, thinking bout the things I like to do, I'm open wide when it comes to freaking you."* She sang softly in my ear. She started grinding to the beat of the music while unbuttoning my shirt. After she stripped my tank top off me, she unhooked her bra and exposed her breast. She ran her tongue from my chest to the bottom of my stomach before unloosening the snap on my pants. By now I was rock hard, and my dick was bulging through my boxers. I stood up to remove my pants and she started sucking on my dick like she was hungry, and I was her last meal. She gazed up at me while she massaged my balls and continued sucking. Shit was driving me crazy. I lifted her up, pulled her thong to the side and slid her on my dick. She bounced up and down on my piece as I held her small waist to keep her steady. We fucked all over the living room before she led me upstairs to her bedroom. She didn't waste no time hopping on top of me. She rhythmically grinded on me until she made herself cum all over my dick. I flipped her around, she got on all fours and arched her back while I beat that pussy up from the back. When I was about to bust, she turned around, took me in her mouth, and sucked the nut out of me. I collapsed on the bed exhausted after fucking her for an hour straight.

"Damn I needed that." She said as she lay aside me trying to cuddle.

"I'm about to hop in the shower. I'll be right out." I slid from under her and went into her connected master bath. I walked out the bathroom and Ivory was curled up in the bed naked and sleep. I covered her up and walked downstairs to find Lil Tray in the kitchen. "Hey son, I've been waiting on you for hours. How long you been here?"

"Sup pops. Long enough to know you and mama been doing

something yall ain't got no business doing." I turned red with embarrassment, the thought of him hearing how I had his mom upstairs hollering made me cringe.

"Did you like the movie." I said to hurry up and switch subjects.

"It was overrated. They showed the best parts of the movie in previews. I could've got it on bootleg."

I shot the breeze with my boy for a while before getting up to leave. It was time to get back to business. I thought I was gonna be able to get to Romell through Ivory but now I gotta find his ass another way. "Aight son, I'll be back to see you soon, I gotta get up outta here. You need anything?"

"Nah pops, I'm good. I'm still spending what you left me last time. But you know my birthday coming up and I want the biggest party ever, on some MTV sweet 16 type of shit..I mean stuff."

"Yea, you betta watch your mouth before you be missing a tooth. And we'll see about this extravagant party. I already just spent a grip on the stuff you wanted for Christmas." I joked before leaving.

I sat in my car to contemplate my next move. I decided to meet up with Monique to see how valuable this information is she got for me. Before I had her ass put out, shit was being done in her apartment so I'm sure she knows something.

14

MONIQUE

Tray agreed to meet me at a restaurant out in Merrillville Indiana, somewhere far from the city but still close. I put on the sexiest outfit in my suitcase. I chose my favorite black spaghetti strap dress with the deep V cut that stopped right below my belly button. I had the girls sitting up right as they were slightly exposed. Since I know Tray likes the finer things in life I wore my most expensive pair of heels, red bottoms. My hair was lifted in a tousled bun and I got my lashes put on after getting a mani and pedi at the nail shop earlier today. After accessorizing, I dabbed on my favorite Rihanna perfume, grabbed my Steve Madden clutch, threw on my coat and headed out the door. It was cold and we had just got five inches of snow. People were out shoveling parking spaces for their car and putting all type of shit down to reserve their spots. I laughed as I looked down the street and saw everything from lawn chairs to baby strollers lined on the curbs holding shoveled spaces.

"HEY TRAY." I said smiling and strutting to the table. He'd already arrived and had a bottle of wine and appetizers by the time I got there. We met at an upscale lounge called Relax and Sip and he was seated in the back of the restaurant in a booth.

"Hey Monica."

"Come on now. You gotta be kidding me."

"Just joking. What's up Monique? I thought this was a business meeting." He said eyeing me from head to toe just like I was hoping he would.

Amari gotta be crazy as hell to be dodging this man. I don't give a fuck what he do for a living, this nigga is fine and paid. "Whaatttt." I dragged the word out flirtaciously as I took off my coat so he can get a better view of what's he been turning down all these years.

"You know what I'm talking about. You look like you dressed for a date miss lady.

This was my first time seeing him without a business suit on in a long time. He was wearing a regular jogging suit and some track Nikes. His dreads looked nappy and his face was scruffy and unshaved. I didn't care because the presence of him alone turned me on. "I um." I hesitated because I wanted to choose my words wisely. "Well Manny hooked me up with a dude name Romell. They used me as a pawn to pick up and deliver big shipments of weight."

He listened intently as he sipped wine. "You know where the weight was coming from?"

"It was always a P.O box. I think it comes from some Columbians."

"So, this Romell cat, where is he from? Where he hang out? Who is he affiliated with?"

He was shooting out questions quicker than I could answer. But I was prepared to tell him everything he needed to know so he could see I'm the type of the bitch he needs, not Amari's lame ass. "From what I know, he's from out of town but he got people on the south side." I indulged everything I knew from beginning to end.

"I need his exact location. You think you can do that?"

"I can do anything you want me to do. But what's in it for me?"

"Give me his location and you will get a huge payday."

"Consider it done."

"Aight. Hit my line when you got some news for me." He said while motioning for the waitress to come over. "This should cover the bill and you can keep the change for your tip." He passed her two hundred dollar bills. With only appetizers and a cheap bottle of wine as his order, she got a hefty tip.

"Okay you'll be hearing from me real soon. But why you leaving so soon?" He was walking towards the exit and I followed right behind him.

"Our meeting is over."

I grabbed his hand and pulled him towards the ladies room. "I got some more information I need to tell you in private, so the meeting isn't quite over." I said as I seductively licked my lips.

"Now what would your friend say knowing that you were coming at me like this?" He asked pulling away.

He'd rejected me one too many times and I was chasing him way before he even knew Amari existed. "What friend? Money is the only friend I have." Being persistent, I seductively licked my lips and exposed the fact that I wasn't wearing any panties under my dress. I cracked open the ladies room door, stood in the doorway, and motioned for him to come over with my finger. To further entice him, I exposed both of my breast. He bucked his eyes and came my way when my naked breasts caused the waiter to drop his whole tray of drinks.

"So, you just gonna make the man lose his job huh? You really crazy." His said shaking his head and chuckling.

"Now that I have your attention, let me show you just how crazy I am." I led him to the handicapped stall, the one with the most space. I cared less about the three uppity looking ass women in the restroom watching me with disgusted looks on their faces. They could mind their fucking business. I'm about to suck his dick and they could watch for all I cared. I locked the door, dropped to my knees and pulled his jogging pants down to his ankles. I slid his dick out his boxers and my mouth started watering at the sight of his gorgeous piece. I started sucking his dick like my life depended on it. I could tell he was enjoying it because his eyes were closed, and his head was tilted back. He grabbed my head to guide it at his rhythm while I worked my magic. I felt him about to nut, so I used my hand to massage his balls while I quickly slid my mouth up and down the tip of his dick. He busted, and I swallowed all of it. Checkmate.

ROMELL MAY HAVE MOVED and changed his number, but I bet his products still moving in the same area. He fucked up letting me in on certain locations. Manny told him I was a whore, but dumb don't fall under that category. I mentally recorded every location I ever met people, every address he had me delivering packages to, and every person he did interactions with. I pulled up on 68th and Normal and parked behind a white van. Romell moves most of his product on the very next block. I noticed his boy Black posted on the porch. Although I was on the next block, I could spot that burnt crispy muthafucka a mile away. Even at night all you see is teeth and eyeballs, so you know it's him. Black was holding shit down over here and Romell stops by every now and then. I had been coming over here for the last few days hoping to catch him with no luck, so I was hoping I would get lucky today. I needed to prove to Tray that thug niggas like him need gansta bitches like me, and I'm definitely that bitch.

Two hours had passed by and still no sign of him. I started to feel sleepy, so I gulped down a 5 hour energy shot. After sitting, for another half hour, I started to leave when I noticed a silver Lincoln MKZ pull up in front of the trap house. Somebody hopped out the passenger seat and sure enough it was that dirty muthafucka. He greeted Black and they walked inside the house. About twenty minutes later, Romell walked out with a backpack and got back in the car. I looked into the rearview mirror to adjust my wig and sunglasses and make sure I was still incognito. I waited until he was at the end of the block before proceeding to follow him. I followed him towards the expressway making sure I stayed two cars behind. After exiting at the same stop we used to get off at to get to his condo, I started reminiscing on the days when things were fresh and new with us. He brought me to this neighborhood and I thought I was in Beverly Hills. I had never been outside those walls at Bricksquare so for me this was Beverly Hills. No litter on the ground, no crackheads standing outside selling loose squares. It was only a handful of churches and not one on every other corner. I used to enjoy the peacefulness of this environment when I needed to escape my life in the projects.

I broke from my daze when I noticed him pull up to one of the most nicest and biggest houses on the block. I immediately shut off my lights and pulled over, close enough to see but far away enough not to be seen. I noticed two cars parked in the driveway, one I didn't recognize. I pulled out my cell phone and double checked to make sure my flash was off before snapping a shot of the house. I also jotted the address down. Mission accomplished I thought to myself. Right as I was proceeding to pull off, I saw Kyra greet him at the door. I lost my cool and got out of the car to go beat the shit out of this broad. I couldn't believe the whole time I been worried and stressing about her ass, she been lamping over here with this nigga. I immediately regained my composure and turned back to get in the car when I thought about Tray. That is not what I came here for, but I will definitely address this shit another time.

15

ROMELL

"What's wrong with you?" I asked Kyra as she walked out of the master bathroom. "Why you throwing up and shit?" I had tucked her away with me when she called saying she and her sister had got put out and she had nowhere to go. If I had to pick a sister, it was a no brainer to pick Kyra. We had got close ever since I took her virginity, so I was more than happy to move her out here with me. She had fell so in love that she even sobered up for a nigga.

"I've been feeling sick lately bae." She cried as she climbed back in our king-size bed.

"Make you an appointment with the doctor, I think you might be pregnant."

"I bet not be pregnant, Monique would really kill me if she found out I'm carrying your child. Especially since you beat hers outta her."

"I wouldn't give a fuck if she found out or not. That bitch can't do shit to me but be mad."

"It ain't you I'm worried about her doing something to. She is my sister remember, that girl ain't never had all her screws. She would try to kill me."

"You're my bitch now and doing something to you is doing something to me. I would reconstruct her face if she ever laid hands on you. Besides, you still haven't talked to her right?"

"No. But I heard through the grapevine that she's been looking for me."

"Even if you talk to her how she gonna know it's mines? Are you gonna tell her?"

"Why would I do that? I'm just saying, what if she does find out?"

"Look let me worry about all that. You just worry about finding a doctor to make sure you're really pregnant. As long as you're with me, ain't shit gonna happen to you." I assured her. I had caught feelings for her over these past few weeks and I planned on making her wifey.

"I already know I'm pregnant because I haven't been on and this is my third time having to use the bathroom already today." She said as walked back in the bathroom.

"You want anything from downstairs while I'm going down?"

"Bring me a glass of orange juice."

I went downstairs to grab a beer out the fridge. I had so much shit on my mind and it was starting to get to me. Shit went from good to bad in a matter of months. I opened the door of my stainless steel smart fridge and grabbed two Coronas. I gulped one down, dropped the bottle in the trash, and headed back upstairs.

"Good afternoon. I'm glad you decided to join us, come have a seat."

I reached on my waist for my gun, but before I could get to it there was a gun pressed against the back of my head. "I wouldn't do that if I were you." The man with the gun said from behind me.

I surrendered and put both my hands up as he guided me to the seat on the couch next to another man already sitting comfortably puffing a cigar. "Who the fuck are yall and what the fuck yall doing in my house?" Shit was crazy because when I moved I didn't give my location to no one.

"Abelardo sent us. You got something for him?"

Abelardo, aka Abel, the plug. My worst nightmare. I knew it was only a matter of time before he came looking for me. "Yall just gone show up to where I lay my head at."

"What did you expect when you've been dodging the bosses calls. You owe him a lot of money." He sat with his legs folded and a condescending smirk on his face. "It's okay Javier, you can put your gun away. I'm sure Romell here will show us good hospitality." He instructed his partner who was still hovering over me with his gun drawn.

"I told him I need more time. The person I'm working with played me out of a lot of cash and that nigga been missing in action."

"Did he put his work in this person you're referring to hands or yours?"

I didn't even answer his question because all he was concerned about was the person they did business with. Abel had fronted me 50 kilos because I assured him that I would move it fast and make him a quick million. I looked out for Manny out of loyalty and because I had more work than me and my team could handle. Plus, our plan to run this city had me more than ready to do business with him. I had already had the south side of the city on lock so connecting with a nigga from the westside was right up my alley. Who was gonna stop us from running shit if we both joined forces? I just connected with the wrong nigga to execute the plan and now I got Abel's psychotic crew on my ass. "Look tell Abel to just give me a lil more time and I will have all of his money. Just don't come barging in my house like this no more, it might not be safe."

"Down boy." He instructed the psycho looking muthafucka who was itching to use his big ass gun. "He's no threat." He chuckled as if he didn't take my threat serious.

I don't know why he sent these burrito eating muthafuckas here like they gone pump fear in my heart. Plus, Abel wants his money and a dead man can't pay him. "If you kill me how am I gonna pay your boss his money." Javier still had his gun pressed into the back of my head disregarding what his partner said.

"What's taking so long with my orange juice?" Kyra said coming around the corner. Once she noticed we had visitors with guns, she turned around to run.

"If you take another step I'll blow your fucking brains out." Javier pulled out a different gun and aimed it towards her while still keeping the other gun to my head.

"Now why didn't you tell me we had more company. Who is this pretty little thing?" His partner wanted to know. "Come come." He said waving Kyra over. "Is there anyone else here we should know about?"

"Nah it's just me and her."

"What's going on Ro? Who are these people?" She looked terrified.

"We were just leaving." The stranger said as he stood up from the sofa. "You might want to get a coat because it looks like you'll be leaving with us." He grabbed Kyra's arm and pushed her towards Javier. "Gag her and put her in the car."

She started kicking and screaming. "Nooooo please don't take me. I'm pregnant...pleeaaaaseee!"

Kyra was getting so wild she caused him to drop the gun he had aimed at me. I pulled my gun from my waist and a shot to my right arm caused me to fall. "One more move and she's dead."

I was holding my arm to apply pressure to the gunshot wound as blood was oozing out. "Aye she ain't got shit to do with this. What you taking her for?"

"Collateral. Since you like to dodge phone calls and feel like you need more time, you now have a reason to answer your phone and move with a sense of urgency. Comprende?"

"You just told me you would protect me. Don't let them take me." Kyra screamed out before Javier stuffed a cloth in her mouth, duck taped it shut, and dragged her out the door.

～

"Give me all the money you made so far and shut down all operations." I hopped on the highway and headed right to the trap house. "Black was there bagging up when I arrived.

"Why? What's going on?" He asked while still putting work on a scale. "I got somebody on the way right now for a pound of this shit."

"I can't really explain right now. I just need you to lay low for a lil while. How much money you got?" I already had a quarter million saved in my personal stash, but I'd been stacking that up since I came home from jail. I worked too hard to just give my shit away because Manny fronted his move.

"It's about $300,000 saved up so far. But I haven't paid the workers yet. And I still gotta get my cut."

"I need all of that right now. It's a matter of life or death. Let everybody know that pay will be delayed this week. You can go ahead and get your cut, but I need the rest."

"So what about this shit we got left?" He asked pointing to the dope he was preparing to set up for the day.

"I need that too." I said while stuffing the money in my duffle bag. "Nah, as a matter of fact, just hold on to that. I don't want to drive with that shit in my car. I might have you to bring that out to my house. I will call and let you know. I gotta get up outta here so be cool my nigga."

16

MANNY

Everything from my balls to the palm of my hands were sweating as I lay in this hard ass bunk thinking about going in front of the judge tomorrow. I was headed to Wisconsin when bullets came flying through my car. For all I knew, that could've been anybody. I survived the accident and only caught a bullet in my right arm. The police searched my car while I was being driven away by the ambulance and found the dope and the cash I'd just gotten from Duke's crib. I left the county hospital in handcuffs and was brought straight to the county jail. Not only did everything I had planned go left, now I might be facing some serious time. Somebody was gonna pay for this shit. The fucked up thing is even if I'm granted a bail I don't have one person to call. Tray was like the only family I ever had but he might be the nigga that's trying to kill me.

"What you in for?" They had just added an inmate to the cell I was in, a young nigga.

"Drugs. Ain't that what all of us in here for?" I had too much shit on my mind and was not in the mood to small talk with no lame looking ass kid.

"I'm in here for attempted robbery." He said it like he wanted a pat on the back or something. "We almost got away but them thirsty ass detectives swerved on us man." I could tell he was somebody's sendoff kid. A lil sorority ass nigga, always doing shit to fit in and prove his self. He was smiling the whole time he was talking with the most bogus grill ever. Nigga teeth was hanging out his mouth. "If our nigga Duke was still alive, he would've been with us and we would've got away. He was a monster behind the wheel."

Hearing him say Duke name got my full attention. He was talking so much I had started to block him out. "He got killed?" I had already figured he was dead, but I didn't stick around long enough to find out for sure. I ain't never seen this mufucka a day in my life so I was wondering how he knew Duke. Duke was born and raised in the square and he was not from our hood.

"Yea. That was my buddy too. We got a lotta money together robbing niggas." He walked towards the bed and climbed in the top bunk still running his mouth. "He told me he was making moves and he didn't need to rob niggas no more. I told that nigga whatever he was getting into he bet not forget about me."

He got quiet and I got up out my bunk to stand up and keep talking. He had drifted off into a deep thought. "How did you know him?"

"We met in high school. He was the only out west nigga in our freshmen class, but he was a cool dude." He had just told me he fucked up and was ready to stop doing whatever he was doing but some punk ass nigga named Manny forced him into it. And now look, he must've knew some shit was finna happen." I hope whoever Manny is get what's coming to him cuz Duke was a good dude and he ain't deserve to go out like that."

"Sorry to hear about your homie."

"It's all good. I heard he went out like a G."

"So, what else he tell you about Manny."

"That he a grimy ass nigga that's double crossing the wrong people. He was geeked up about working with him at first. Gone tell me he was thru robbing mufuckas for a living because he was finna start swimming with the big fish."

"What's your name?" His lil goofy ass needed to be silenced. I warned Duke dumb ass not to tell no mufucka about our plan just like I told him don't start spending money and being flashy yet. That was his downfall, a young nigga that didn't listen. Ain't no telling who else ears this lil goofy dude been putting my name in.

"Everybody call me Rev."

"Come down here Lil Rev. I need to look at you when I say what I'm about to say."

He tried to act like he was tough. "You can tell me whatever you got tell me while I'm right here, fuck you on my nigga?"

"You never asked me my name, I'm Manny. Nice to meet you Rev, now get your lil goofy ass out that bunk before I snatch your water faucet mouth ass down."

The look on his face was priceless, you would've thought I just told him I'm the devil himself. He slowly got up and climbed down and sat on my bunk. "I swear I didn't say nothing about this to nobody. I promised Duke I wouldn't say nothing." He looked terrified.

"You ain't even know what the fuck my name was, and I know your whole life story. You think I believe you ain't been running your mouth like a bitch?" I grabbed him by the neck and pinned his head into the bed. "You bet not ever let my name roll off your tongue again." I pushed his head further down and he squealed in pain. "Real niggas don't run around talking like bitches. But since you acting like a bitch, I'm about to make you my bitch."

"Man, you crazier than I thought." He muffled out trying to break away from my grip.

I snatched his pants down with my free hand and put my knee in his back. "You better bite the bed because if you scream I'm gonna choke the life out of you."

I loved pussy just like the next nigga, but I needed a man every now and then. I was raped by my uncle when I was eleven years old. He'd just gotten out of jail and came to live with my grandmother who was raising me at the time. He was a big cocky nigga who'd spent most of his childhood in prison. So, he was used to taking advantage of lil dudes like me. I knew what it felt like to be fucked before I even knew what pussy felt like. It went on until I was fourteen years old

because I had been too embarrassed to tell anyone about it. But I'd
finally got fed up and had just gotten my hands on my first pistol. I
waited patiently one night for him to come in my room. He came in
and locked the door like he always did when he was about to rape
me. My grandma had fallen ill and was on hospice, so she could do
nothing. She couldn't even hear my screams. I had the gun under my
pillow. When he instructed me to move the covers, I reached under
my sheet, pulled out the gun, and held it to his face. I told him I was
the one who would be giving orders this time. I stood behind him
and played with my dick until it got hard and ripped into his asshole
the same way he'd been doing me. Although he liked fucking boys
he'd never been fucked. After I felt like I'd tortured him enough, I let
off two shots. One in his dick and one in his head. It was my first time
having sex and my first time killing. I remember being in awe looking
at the blood spill from my uncle's lifeless body. At that moment, I
knew I'd always get a thrill out of killing. What I didn't know is that
I'd also have a side of me that liked men no matter how much I tried
to fight the urge. I never told nobody about what happened to me as a
kid. I knew I'd never be respected on the streets if mufuckas knew
about that side of me.

FEET SHACKLED AND HANDCUFFED, the sheriff escorted me down the
hall that led to the courtroom. My stomach was in knots thinking
about my freedom being in the hands of another judge. I spent most
of my teen years incarcerated for murdering my uncle. I've only been
free for a year and I was not ready to go back. I was hoping for some
leniency since I caught that case as a juvenile. The closer we got to
the courtroom, the more nervous I became. It felt like I was about to
shit in my pants. My case was up next and the first thing I noticed
when I walked through the door is the same white muthafucka who
sentenced me to ten years. Even though I was a rape victim, that
racist honkey showed me no sympathy. He'd aged horribly over the
years. His skin was pale, and his eyes were sunken in his wrinkly old

face. He ran his fingers through his silver head of hair as he read over the case documents. I observed a court room full of blonde head attorneys and young white lawyers. Aside from the folks who was sitting in as observers and the criminals, the only other black people were the clerk and the sheriff. This racist ass shit, I thought to myself, I'm fucked.

"Raise your right hand." "Do you swear that the testimony you're about to give is the truth the whole truth, and nothing but the truth."

"Yes."

"The judge will now hear your case."

"Mr. Hayes, after all these years, we meet again." He acted like he was happy to see me standing in front of him again.

Just like I knew the minute I laid eyes on Judge Brenner, I was shit out of luck. He had a reputation for fucking over black males and sentencing us to the max in ninety percent of his cases. I left with a new court date and a denied bail. The difference between then and now is I can pay for a lawyer so I'll be ready on my next appearance.

Carver was in town to bring CJ back but told me he had some business to handle so I'd have to pick CJ up from his mom´s house. That's some new shit too, this bitch must got some type of control over him because he never had a problem coming to my house. I pulled into his mom, Mrs. Vita´s, driveway anxious to see my son. It had been two weeks since he'd been gone and that was the longest he'd ever been away from me. I hadn't seen his mom in a while and I was actually looking forward to seeing her. We were always close, and she was like a second mom to me.

"I'm glad Carver met you. I can't remember when the last time he was so happy."

"I fell in love with him the minute I met him. It was like love at first sight. I want to tell Amari thank you for sending me my husband. I don't know how she let him go."

"That's her loss. My son did everything for that girl and as soon as he fell on hard times she kicked him to the curb." Mrs. Vita was having a conversation with her new daughter in law. I stopped shy of where they were seated because I heard my name and wanted to ear hustle.

"She must was using him from the beginning. Because if you love your man, you don't leave him when he fall off a little bit. I don't have anything against her, but she comes across as money hungry and boogie."

"Baby she come from the projects, ain't a uppity bone in her body. When my son first brought her home, she ain't have nothing. He took her off the bus and put her in her first car. He even moved her out of her mother's house and put her and CJ in that house she in now."

"Really? Wow. And that's the thanks he got in return?"

"Ole ungrateful ass. But that's ok, because he lost her and found something better. Plus, I been wanting another grandchild for the longest. Her eggs must be rotten because Carver said they tried many times to make another baby."

That Mexican bitch started laughing and rubbing her belly like some shit was funny. "Well it was definitely her because you have a grandbaby on the way now."

"I can't wait either. I just hope it's a girl because I know she's going to be the prettiest little mixed baby with long pretty hair."

My blood was boiling at this point. I been knowing this old hag since I was a teenager. She been knowing this bitch for 2.5 seconds and she sitting here dogging me out to this hoe. "Mrs. Vita I don't appreciate you in here talking about me and telling all my business to this chick."

"Hey Amari. How did you get in here." She was shocked to see me standing there.

"CJ let me in."

"I told that boy about opening doors. I'm gone beat his lil grown butt."

"He knew it was me because he was in the window when I pulled in the driveway." She wasn't gonna do a damn thing to my son. The way I was feeling at the moment, she better hope she see him again.

"And wasn't nobody talking about you. We was talking about her baby."

"I was standing behind that wall for the longest." I said pointing to wall that separated the kitchen from the living room. "I heard everything you said and it's cool. I never knew you were so phony."

She started getting defensive and yelling. "I wasn't telling her your business. She know all there is to know about you already."

"She don't know shit about me not being able to get pregnant. And unless she pillow talking in the bed with her man about me, she don't know my fucking business." I had never disrespected her, but I was pissed. Not only did I feel betrayed, but she gone look me right in my eyes and lie to me.

"First of all, don't nobody be thinking about you when I'm in the bed my man." She interrupted.

I went from ten to fifty. This bitch ain't have shit to do with this. "Am I talking to you? I walked up in her face so close I was hoping she could smell the pancakes I ate for breakfast on my breath. "If you don't mind your business I'll knock your Mexican ass back across the border."

"I ain't worried about it." She said backing up and walking away. She ain't want these problems. She might try to talk and act like she black, but I'll beat her ass and remind her who the fuck she is.

"Yea you better stay in your lane."

"Amari just get CJ and leave. I don't need this drama in my house."

"So, you putting me out too. Yea ok. It'll be a cold day in hell before you see me or my son again with yo phony ass." I stormed in the foyer and yelled up the stairs for CJ to come down and left that lady house before I said something to her that would've made Carver hate me for the rest of his life. Mother in laws are phony as hell. They love whoever their son loving on at the moment.

My mother was anxious to see her grandson, so I decided to go to her house before going home.

"McDonalds! Mommy I want a happy meal." CJ said pointing to a McDonalds arch that was all the way off the expressway. I hate them damn arches because kids can spot those things from miles away.

"Your grandma didn't feed you this morning."

"I didn't want that stuff she cooked. She cooked bacon and I don't eat pork."

I busted out laughing. This lil boy done been down there with his no pork eating daddy for two weeks and all of a sudden he don't he don't eat pork. "Since when?" I asked watching him through the rearview.

"My daddy said pork isn't good for you. You should stop eating it too ma."

He had the most serious look on his face like he was really trying to persuade me. "Pigs are nasty animals."

I was cracking up. This lil boy mind was like a sponge, he soaked up everything. "You and your daddy."

"Ma stop laughing. I'm fo'weal." He pronounced all his R letters like W's. "I don't want you to get sick."

"Okay baby. I'll think about it." I made a mental note to curse Carver's ass out about this one. He not gonna stop me from eating my bacon.

After stopping and getting him a chicken nugget happy meal, I stopped for gas and then went to my mother's house.

"Motherrrrr." I sang as I walked in with my key. Soon as I walked in the smell of my mother's infamous smoked meat and black-eyed peas hit my nose and I instantly regretted eating that damn burger from McDonalds. She had to be warming up her New Year's dinner because it was tradition for her to cook black eyed peas on the first day of every year.

CJ took off his shoes and coat and ran right to his granny's room. He was crazy about her. "Gwanny!!" He said as he hugged her legs.

"Hey baby. You want to see what Granny got you for Christmas." My mom was mad I let him spend the holidays out of town.

"Yes!" He said jumping up and down.

She grabbed his hand and led him to the living room. She still had her Christmas tree and holiday decorations up. She refused to take it down until her grandbaby came home to open his gifts. "Come on baby."

"Mama I need you to keep him, I'm going out tonight."

"He just came home and you ready to drop him off already? Where you going?"

"Me and Monique going out." I was hanging out with Tray but

didn't want to tell her that. I wasn't ready to tell her about him because I wasn't sure of him myself. Plus, I just didn't need her in my business giving her cut throat opinions.

"Get a garbage bag first baby before you start opening your gifts." He had a tree full of unwrapped gifts and my mama was anal about keeping her space clean. Growing up I had to do the same thing, unwrap my gifts and put the paper in the garbage bag as I go. I laughed on the inside thinking about how she was still stuck in her ways. "You starting to hang out with that damn Monique a little too much now. It's like she couldn't wait to see you and Carver break up."

"What are you talking about ma? That's so far from the truth."

"I done told you before just because you grew up with that girl don't make her your friend. I might be dead and gone when you realize the things I be trying to tell you. I ain't made it to this age for nothing. Just watch your so-called friend."

"What you want me to do? Sit in the house sad and depressed?" She was about to blow me. This is exactly why I don't like telling her shit. "She's been helping me keep my mind off how much my life has fallen apart over the past few months. If it wasn't for her I'd be in the house drowning in liquor and weed all miserable."

"And what you doing now? In the streets drowning in weed and liquor?" She asked sarcastically. "Partying every weekend and doing all the things you said you had grown out of?"

"I'm still young, I'm supposed to be enjoying my life ma. Ain't nothing wrong with partying every now and then."

"I just wish you had the kind of friend that wants as much out of life as you. I know this gone sound cliché' but you are the company you keep. You shouldn't have nobody around you that doesn't have the same goals in life as you because they'll keep you at a standstill. If you want to be successful in life, you need to surround yourself with successful people that you can learn something from. That so-called friend of yours don't want nothing out of life but some drug dealer's dick and a high."

I shook my head and laughed at her last statement. "Ma don't talk about my friend."

"You'll learn one day, hopefully sooner than later. That girl always been jealous of you."

"Look Ma. Gwanny got me my favorite!!" CJ shot over towards me holding up his favorite Paw Patrol toy with the biggest smile on his face.

Before I could respond he darted to the bedroom with his favorite gift. He didn't even bother to open anything else after he opened that one. I was glad he interrupted our conversation though because I definitely didn't stop over here to get lectured today. "Ma I gotta go. I need to stop and find me some shoes to wear tonight and start getting ready. I'll talk to you later." I grabbed a plastic bag from under the sink and put my containers of food inside before kissing my mom on the cheek.

"Okay, just remember what I said and be careful hanging out with that little slut." She said as she wiped down the kitchen counters. That lady is a trip.

AFTER PICKING up the prettiest pair of knee length Emilio Pucci boots, I went home to prepare for my date with Tray. I had been ignoring him long enough and even though I told myself he was cut off, I couldn't get his ass off my mind.

Soon as I crossed the threshold the smell of weed and black and milds slapped me in the face. I was livid. "Mo didn't I tell you there was no smoking in the house."

"I know but I figured since CJ wasn't here it would be ok. Plus, it's cold as hell in that garage."

Letting her move in was a huge mistake. She don't follow none of the rules I set in place and she thinks her name is on the damn lease or something. She done got too comfortable. "That's why you supposed to turn on the heat when you go in there and CJ is back home. I just left him at my mother's house."

"Okay, I promise I won't break any more of your rules friend."

"How much longer do you think you need to be here?" As much

as I wanted to, I just couldn't bring myself to put her out. Her life has always been rough with nobody really showing her unconditional love. Sometimes I feel like I'm the only family she has. That's why I've never turned my back on her.

"Not much longer. I just had a very important meeting. As a matter of fact, I'm going to pay the security deposit on my apartment tomorrow."

"That's good friend but who you have a business meeting with? A strip club owner? All your titties hanging all out that dress." I said giving her a onceover.

"No. It was an important business meeting with a man that just helped me with the down payment to my new place." She said flashing a wad of money. "And you know a girl gotta use what she got to get what she want." She said quoting her favorite whore line from players club. She been using that damn line since she saw that movie all those years ago.

I shook my head. "Girl you are too much for me."

"What? Ain't nothing wrong with sucking a lil dick to get what you want in life. I know bitches that suck dick every day for free." She plopped down on the couch and continued talking. "I'm so forreal. I gotta hurry up and hit a lick too because thirty right around the corner. And you know these dudes like em with milk still behind the ears."

"Speaking of young girls, what's up with your sister?"

The smile she was wearing instantly faded away at the mention of her sister. She cut her eyes at me and just stared for about thirty seconds. "I found that bitch Kyra. And she ain't no sister of mine. You'll never guess where that lil bitch been this whole time."

"Where."

"Laid up in the burbs with Romell ass."

"Girl get the fuck outta here." I couldn't believe what I was hearing. That's the dirtiest shit you can do to your own sister.

"I got something for her ass though. She should know better than to cross me like that. And I found out he was only using me. He used me for what I was good for at the time, let me go, and cuffed my sister. But payback is a bitch."

I wanted to hear about the latest events of her life and tell her about the latest happenings in mine, but I was running behind for my date with Tray. "Girl you got a full plate. But don't do nothing crazy. Ain't neither one of em worth the stress."

"I'm whooping Kyra's ass on sight!" She had a demonic look on her face. "But I got something better planned for that nigga Romell."

I couldn't do nothing but shake my head. It wasn't no sense in trying to talk her out of whatever she had planned. She could be an evil bitch when she wanted to and the streets have turned her into someone I don't know. She was always crazy and wild, but it seems like those years I was shacked up in the house with my family, she'd gotten worse. I was the only piece of sanity she had in her life and since I hadn't been there to talk her out of doing crazy shit, ain't no telling what she's been into. "Just be careful friend. I'm finna go out with Tray in a minute so I'll talk to you later."

"Where you off to now? Yall always doing something." I heard a twinge of jealousy in her voice, something I'd never picked up before.

All I could hear is my mother's voice playing through my head, *that girl always been jealous of you.* I immediately dismissed the thought. "I don't know yet. He just told me to wear something comfortable, preferably gym shoes. Shit, sounds like we going hiking or something."

"Well, have fun. See you when you get back."

18

TRAY

"If the leaves on the trees around this muthafucka blow the wrong way I want to know about it." I was at Bricksquare in the 2103 building having a meeting with the new people I put in place. I got rid of every pack man and any other muthafucka that I felt crossed me. "Manny ain't in charge of shit no more. The only person yall answer to from this point on is me."

"I can make sure these niggas in order boss man. Let me take some of that load off you." Choppa was front and center at the meeting with me ready to chop some niggas heads off after I filled him in on what had been going on. He begged me to let him handle Manny personally. But that's something I gotta do myself.

"I'll let you know if I need you to slide through. But for now, I only trust my own eyes." I didn't mind Choppa handling my light weight but until I handle these niggas that crossed me, I was gonna get my own hands dirty. "Any word on that nigga Manny's release date?"

"Last time I checked he was denied bail and scheduled for another court date. That nigga got caught with 10 kilos and 150,000 in cash. They about to slam his ass. I don't think he getting released no time soon." Rio, one of the packmen who was in tune with Manny and his case replied.

"When he go to court?"

"I gotta find out the exact date. I'll have my girl to look it up and let you know asap." Rio was good for getting any information I needed legally because his girl is a defense attorney. "You know they say that nigga a fruit cake,°q right?"

"Who Manny? Nah, that nigga stayed with different hoes."

"Man, they say he in there snatching up young niggas asses." Rio said cringing.

"That nigga been gay this whole time huh?" Just when I thought I knew everything there was to know about him, I didn't know the man at all. "That's some sick ass shit." I said trying to dismiss the image of him being with a man. "Aight, hit my line when you get an update on his case. In the meantime, back to business as usual." After sliding through and checking in on the other buildings, me, Fendi, and Choppa hopped in his Chevy and peeled out the parking lot.

"So, she said he moving his work in Englewood?" Choppa was anxious to make it to the south side and he was out for blood.

We pulled up close to the address Monique had given me. It was dark outside, and we were dressed in all black. Choppa popped the trunk and this nigga had enough guns to supply an army. We strapped up and walked towards the house. Fendi posted up by the back door and me and Choppa walked to the front of the house. Choppa popped the lock off quietly and we made our way in.

"If you make a sound I'mma put a bullet through your adams apple. Who else is in here?" I had my gun pressed against some black ass niggas neck while Choppa checked to make sure no one else was inside.

"Man, who the fuck are you? I'm alone."

"I'm your worst nightmare." I butted him in the mouth with my gun knocking out two teeth in the process. "I'm only gonna ask you this one time. Where the fuck is the money?"

"What money? I swear I don't have shit." He said while spitting and trying to stop from swallowing his blood.

That was the wrong answer. I shot him in both his arms. "The money that nigga you work for stole from me."

"AAAgggggghhhh." He hugged himself trying to put pressure on the gunshot wounds in his arms. "He came a few weeks ago and took everything. The money and the work. He told me operations had to be shut down and I haven't heard from him since. I swear to you man."

"What's his location?"

"He lives somewhere in Hickory Hills, but I don't know the address. Please don't kill me."

"Give him a message for me. Tell him I said every dollar he made at Bricksquare is mine and I want my shit by yesterday."

"THEY SAID he'll be released in an hour." Ivory had just posted bail for Manny, 250k. I pulled a few strings to get him a bail and posted the money. It had been over a month and his case kept getting continued and I had grown impatient.

"Alright. Where is your ride?"

"She should be pulling up in a few minutes."

"Okay, shoot me a text when you make it home. Thanks for everything babymama. I love you."

"Why you acting like this the last time you gone see me. That sounds final as hell."

I couldn't do nothing but laugh. I don't tell her I love her that often, but I felt like she needed to hear it. "Cut it out Ivory, I'll talk to you later." I kissed her on the cheek and she exited the car.

An hour later Manny came walking out with his tan pants and white tee shirt on and a cheesy ass grin on his face. It felt like deja vu because almost a year ago today I was picking him up from a different prison. Then I felt feelings of excitement and happiness watching him walk out those prison gates. Now he looked like a snake slithering in grass and all I felt was feelings of anger and hate. He walked towards a car with a lady in the driver's seat. She got out the car and greeted him with a hug. I couldn't make out who she was from this far back, but I watched in disgust as he grasped her ass and tongued her down. If only she knew she was happily kissing a nigga who probably just took his dick out another niggas ass.

I followed them for a little bit over an hour before they pulled up to a small house in Griffith Indiana. Before that nigga's feet hit the concrete I open fired on the car. I got out the car to get closer and make sure I completed the job this time and so that nigga could see my face. As I got closer, the female was nearly unconscious slumped over the steering wheel bleeding from her neck. Too bad for her she had caught his bullet and would sit in that car and bleed to death. Manny was still alive trying to drag himself towards the door of house. I stood over him and imprinted my timberland boot in his face to stop him from moving.

"You thought you was gonna get away with that shit you pulled? I made you who you are, and you decided cross me?" Even though I knew what it was, a part of me still wanted to hear what this nigga had to say. I once considered him my brother and never thought the time would come that we'd come to this.

"Tray, it was a plot against that nigga. I was gonna tell you about it. I just had to set it up first. That nigga got his hands on a lot of work." He mumbled from under my foot. I took my foot off his face and aimed my gun towards the middle of his forehead. "Hear me out, don't kill me, just hear me out." He pleaded. "It's plenty more where that came from. He got work in another state and his connect be giving him a good play. We could link up and take everything."

"Why should I trust your snake ass? You ain't loyal to me, and now you trying to cross another nigga that's trying to help your bitch made down low ass. I don't need his plug, his money or his drugs. All those years you were gone I was stacking and coming up with a plan to retire from the drug game before my thirtieth birthday. I'm through with this shit. I was just about to pass the torch to you anyway." Before I could say another word the sound of police sirens snapped me back to what I was there for. I spit in his face and put two bullets through his forehead before fleeing the scene.

19

ROMELL

"Come on Black we gotta go. Leave him."

"I can't just leave him like this."

More shots let off and a bullet came so close to my face I could smell the heat from it. Firing back, I ran faster towards the black surburban truck that waited for us. "Lets's go!" I screamed at him. Black finally let his cousin's lifeless body go and hopped in the truck and we sped out of the parking lot.

"Fuck man!" Black was outraged as he punched the dashboard to let off some frustration.

We had just robbed three of the buildings at Bricksquare and lost one of our soldiers in the process. I got Tray's message, but I don't fear no man. He had to pay for what he did to my guy. I felt bad because I got him involved in something he ain't have nothing to do with. And now he just lost his closest cousin. "I'm sorry about Mac. Them niggas gone pay for that." The war started when Manny got me involved with Tray. But I got enough soldiers on my team to take out that whole fucking project. Robbing the buildings was just what I needed to pay off Abel and get them off my back. Plus, I needed Kyra back at home, so she can carry my kid peacefully.

"You got a location on Tray?" Black asked as he was fighting to hold back tears.

"Not yet, but I know how to find out."

~

KYRA SAT on the bench looking dirty and cold. After I dropped the money off, Abel had his men to drop her off at a park where I had to pick her up from. Her hair was roughly tousled all over her head. She had on the same gown she was wearing when they snatched her out of the house. Instead of gaining weight like she should have been during her pregnancy, she looked like she'd dropped a lot of pounds.

"About time."

"Hey Kyra. You okay?" I embraced her, but her body odor was so strong it caused me to frown up and step back.

"Am I ok? What the fuck kind of question is that? What the hell took you so long to come get me?"

"You think I just got a million dollars laying around the mutha-fucking house?"

"You got plenty of money. Ain't no reason I should've been held captive for damn near a whole month."

"I could've been came and got you then we wouldn't have shit. I had to make some moves and that shit took time. You better be glad you pregnant with my baby or I would've left your ass to rot." I had never treated her bad, but I was losing my patience. Ain't nothing worse than an ungrateful bitch. I had just suffered a million dollar loss so she oughta be happy I didn't let Javier have his way with her. I been so nice to her she forgot how fast I'll check her.

"Forreal Ro? That's how you feel. I got kidnapped for something I ain't have nothing to do with. But it's cool. Just take me home. I need to shower and feed my unborn child." She bundled her arms inside her coat and walked away with an attitude."

"I'm sorry Kyra. You right." I said pacing behind her. Something about this damn girl got me feeling soft. I'm known for knocking bitches upside their head and I ain't touched her yet. "What you want to eat?"

We stopped by a Chinese restaurant and she ordered her favorite, Mongolian Shrimp with a few egg rolls. Soon as I passed her the food she tore into the bag as if she hadn't eaten in months. "They wasn't feeding you?"

"I need a drink."

"You need what? Don't play with me. I wish you would think about that shit while you carrying my child."

"I don't give a fuck about this baby right now. I'm stressed the fuck out." She cracked open her can of 7up and gulped the whole thing down. Reacting to the acid from the soda, she burped loudly as she continued talking. "My life just flashed before my eyes. I didn't know if I would make it out of that situation alive." She folded the container of food and put in back inside the plastic bag before placing it on the backseat. She turned to look out the passenger window and I noticed a tear falling down her cheek. "I was raped."

I unconsciously pressed my foot down on the gas pedal causing me to speed. I was enraged. I was the only nigga whose dick had ever been inside her. "They wasn't supposed to put their fucking hands on you. That was part of the agreement."

"Well they had their way with me and I feel nasty, disgusted, and ashamed." Tears were now pouring from her eyes.

I sped thru traffic swerving in and out of lanes trying to wrap my mind around what she was telling me. I blasted the radio to tune out her cries because I hated this feeling of not having control over certain situations. And a nigga violating my girl was definitely one of them. We pulled up to the house and the first thing I noticed was the glass on the side of the door was broken. "Stay in the car." I pulled out my gun and walked into the house quietly. It was dark so I flicked the light switch. The scene before my eyes caused to me to throw up instantly. Black and a few of his guys were laid across the living room dead with their hands and feet chopped off lying beside them. On the cocktail table was the brick I assumed they used to break in. I walked around the bodies and made my way to the table because I noticed a piece of paper under the brick. I scooted the brick off the paper with my gun and it was a bold black square drawn on the paper. A brick and a square, bricksquare. I got Tray's message loud and clear.

20

AMARI

"I s Tray here?" I showed up at his door ready. I had on my long ankle length coat with nothing on under it. Just heels and a coat. However, the half-naked Hispanic chic that opened the door instantly threw off my mood.

She blocked my way by stretching her arms out to the other side of the door. "Excuse me. Who are you?"

She had the nastiest attitude as she eyed me from head to toe. I started to open my coat to give this bitch something to look at since she was staring so hard. "I'm looking for Tray. Is he here?" I didn't feel the need to explain who I was. The question was who the fuck is she.

"He's sleeping and I'm not gonna disturb him." She turned around to go back inside and tried to close the door behind her.

I could tell she was some type of maid because she had on an apron. But when she turned around and I noticed she was wearing nothing but lace thongs under it, I knew she was more than just some fucking maid. Tray got some explaining to do. Before I knew it, I pushed her to the side and barged up the stairs to his room. "Wake up Tray!" I was jerking him back and forth since he seemed to be in a deep sleep. "Tray!"

"What..what." His eyes were still closed so I walked over to the window to pull back the curtains. "Turn that light off." He was using his hands to block the sun that came beaming thru the windows.

"Wake up Tramaine. Who the fuck is that half naked Mexican bitch that's giving me a nasty attitude."

"Hey Mari, calm down. She's not Mexican, she's Cuban."

"I wouldn't give a fuck if she was Arabian. What the hell is she doing here?" I tightened my coat up to make sure I didn't expose myself. Apparently, he done seen enough naked ass anyway. "And Don't tell me to calm down. I been blowing your phone up all morning. Then I get over here to see this. Who is she Tray?"

"Who Maricella?" He sat up yawning and stretching acting all nonchalant.

"I guess that's her name. Why she don't have on no clothes and what is she doing here?"

"That's my housekeeper."

"I guess yall fucking or something."

"Man, ain't nobody fucking her. What the fuck you yelling for?"

"You got this hoe prancing around with no clothes on early in the morning and you telling me to calm down. How come I don't know about her. I hate these kind of surprises." Ever since I been dealing with him it's been nothing but problems. I been getting random friend requests from bitches on facebook, anonymous phone calls with bitches just calling and hanging up. And now this. He must've made sure this bitch was nowhere around every time I came over because I never laid eyes on her.

"You want me to tell her to put some clothes on?" He asked as if I was getting on his nerve.

"Naw. I want you to tell that tramp her services are no longer needed."

"What? You want me to fire my maid? You tripping."

"It's her or me Tray. That bitch just disrespected me, and she needs to leave and never come back or I will."

"Are you gonna do everything she does for me? Cook, clean, run errands...

"You know what." I said cutting him off. "Don't even worry about it." I couldn't believe he was sitting here debating with me about this whore. I stormed towards the bedroom door.

"Where you going? Get back over here."

"Shut the fuck up talking to me. I'm leaving." I stepped in the hallway and to my disgust she was standing her funky ass right there with a smirk on her face. She had heard the whole argument and was pleased that I didn't get my way. Before I knew it, I hauled off and slapped that condescending ass grin off her face and proceeded to whoop her ass. I was sick of these Mexican bitches anyway. First my babydaddy no habla English ass bitch wanna give me lip, now her. I took all my frustration out on her as I flung her on the floor, sat on top of her, and pounded her in her face. "Yea. I don't see that smile now." I said as I continued beating her ass. She didn't even try to fight back. She just used her hands as a shield to protect her face. I drew my arm back to continue swelling up her face, but I felt Tray grab my hand and lift me off her. "Let me go! Grab that bitch." I was kicking and squirming trying to break free of his grasp.

"What the fuck has gotten into you? It's too early for this shit." Tray said trying to restrain me.

Maricella had got up and we both were standing there, asshole naked. "Now get the fuck out before I drag you down the stairs and put you out."

"I don't gotta go nowhere until Tray tells me to leave." Face swollen, busted lip, and a black eye, yet she still felt the need to talk shit.

"Get dressed and leave Maricella."

"But papi." She said about to plead her case.

"Papi? I got your papi." I tried in vain to break from his strong grip. "You heard what the fuck he just said."

"Just leave, your services are no longer needed. You can keep the car and I'll send your belongings and last check in the mail."

"You should've stayed in your lane chica." I said in my best Hispanic accent as she embarrassingly walked towards the spiral stairwell with the most pathetic look on her face.

After escorting her off the property, he came back upstairs to join me. "Damn baby. You just showed out." He said as he walked into the master bathroom.

I was standing in front of his marble double sink using the mirror to fix my hair. "You got me acting like this. This is so far out of my character."

"I got you acting like that huh?"

I was still irritated and I just wanted to go but he asked me not to and of course I stayed. "You know you do. Where the hell you been hiding her?"

"I ain't been hiding her, yall just never crossed paths before now."

"I guess that's pure coincidence?"

"It must be because I don't got nothing to hide from you baby."

I cut my eyes at him because I knew he was lying. He just didn't expect me to pop up over here today, so he didn't have time to get rid of the bitch. "So, you wasn't fucking your hired help?" I asked knowing the answer already. If her maid uniform wasn't evident enough, the way she acted towards me was proof. Bitches don't get in their feelings over somebody they're not fucking.

"What I tell you? I chose you. If I still wanted to play the field that's what I could've did. Now can you let that go. She's gone and at your request she's never coming back. Ok baby?" He said as he walked behind me and pressed his bare skin against my naked body. "Seeing that side of you turned me on. My dick hard as hell."

I hated that I couldn't resist this man. I used to consider myself strong, but I have accepted so much of his lies and bullshit since I've been in this relationship that I have to question myself these days. I stared at our reflections in the mirror and we looked damn good together. "She bet not come back on this property unless she want to get her ass beat again."

He walked towards the shower and stood in front of the entrance looking like a Calvin Klein model with just his CK boxers on and his manhood bulging through. "Come take a shower with me."

~

AFTER WE STEAMED up the shower and got dressed, Tray asked me to go with him to check in on his businesses. We pulled up to the corner of Roosevelt and Kostner and entered a gas station.

"The only thing better than drug money is oil money. Welcome to my latest business venture." Tray was proud as we walked towards the entrance of the store.

It was still under construction and nothing but yellow hats were moving around drilling and hammering. "When will it be open?"

"This summer and I can't wait. This is the first of many. I plan on having a chain of these boys."

"A black man with a chain of gas stations? This is brilliant."

He opened the door so he could give me a tour of the inside. I laughed to myself at his excitement. He was acting like a kid in the candy store. He pointed to an area in the corner where the workers were installing shelves, "That's where the household supplies and stuff gonna go. The freezers and refrigerators are gonna be lined up against that wall."

"I'm so happy for you bae. It's so inspiring watching you fulfill your dreams."

"Yea, this is my way out the game." He grabbed my hand and led me back to the car. "You ready for our next stop?" He said as he opened the passenger door and helped me in.

"I'm ready when you are. But, where we going?"

"I told you I wanted to show you what I've been doing with my time over the past few months."

"Well let's get to the next stop then."

We got back in his Tesla and headed South towards Hyde park. I thought to myself he must got a restaurant because this area is filled with them. Driving pass several restaurants reminded me of how hungry I was. "Can we stop and get something to eat? I'm hungry."

"What you got a taste for?"

"I want some jerk chicken. What kind of spots they got around here?"

"The best jerk chicken spot in the city is on 79th and Halsted, Jerk Villa. We could go there after we leave here."

"I know about Jerk Villa. I just don't feel like waiting another hour before I eat. They take all day in there even if you call your order in."

"Well Uncle joes is around the corner from where we going, so place an order with them."

I pulled out my cell phone to google the number to the restaurant. "You want anything?"

"Nah, I'm good."

We pulled in front of a store front on 52nd and Drexel. The for rent sign was still in the window. "This is a nice lil spot." I said checking out the surroundings. It was in a strip mall right next to a nail salon, a bank, and a few restaurants. "Whatever you plan on opening right here people definitely won't have to worry about parking." The parking lot was huge and the foot traffic in the strip mall was heavy. A perfect place to open a new business.

"It's a perfect location for the business that's about to be open." He said as he put the car in park and grabbed his cell phone from the cupholder. "Let's go see what the inside look like. This one isn't under construction anymore, so you get to see the finished product."

His deep voice was so commanding, and he just had this presence about himself that screamed boss. I didn't want to admit it, but Monique was right when she teased me saying he got my nose wide open. When he walks in the room I get butterflies in my stomach. As smart as I am, he sometimes makes me stumble over my words as I get lost in his trance. He had me feeling like a teenager who had just got her first kiss and I loved every minute of it. I had sworn to myself that Carver would be the last street nigga that I would ever deal with. So, I don't know how I let this criminal sweep me off my feet. But I couldn't get enough of him. I had went on a few dates here and there when me and Carver were going through our breakup. I went out with a few guys who weren't "from the streets" but they bored me to death. Ciara was right when she said I tried that good boy game but this dope boy turning me on.

He grabbed my hand and placed a set of keys inside. "Can you unlock the door for me? I'm coming right behind you. I gotta take this call."

"Okay." I unlocked the door and the alarm scared me causing me to jump back.

Tray walked up laughing. "Stop being so scary. It's only an alarm."

"Ain't nothing funny. You should've told me it was an alarm. That just scared me half to death."

"The way you was just whooping Maricella, I didn't think you had a scared bone in your body." He was still tickled.

"Shut up before I get mad about that bitch. I was trying to forget about that shit. But you had to bring it up."

He grabbed me from behind and covered my mouth with his hand to shut me up. He walked me in the door after disabling the alarm. "This is why I told you to quit your job."

I was speechless. Tray had rented out this space for my hair salon and had already got it fixed up. There were ten booths all decked out with the prettiest plush girly decorations. The color scheme was silver and white with purple highlights, my favorite color. I was in awe as I noticed he had the first booth personalized with my name engraved over the mirror. "Wow." That was all I could manage to say as I took in what I was looking at. Since I was a little girl I dreamed of owning my own salon. To have someone basically hand it to me on a silver platter was more than I could ask for. I got emotional and my eyes started to water up.

"Wait hold the tears baby. Look around."

I took a tour of the whole salon. The shampoo bowls, the receptionist area, the waiting area, everything was nice. He had satellite radio hooked up with speakers embedded in the ceilings. Talk about surround sound. "Thanks bae. I don't know what I can ever do to repay you for this."

"Oh yea. I know what you can do."

I put my hand on my hip and looked at him like he was crazy. "What?"

He hit a button on the remote that sat on one of the booths and H-Town's classic song playing through the speakers.....*The sweetest woman in the world, can be the meanest woman in the world, if you make her that way......It's a thin line between love and hate.* "I know I've taken you through a lot over this past year. I saw you go from being happy to being fed up. But I promise you from here on out I will bring you nothing but happiness. So, if you don't mind, what you can do for me is let me be your husband." He got down on one knee and pulled out a box from his pocket. "Will you marry me?" He asked as he opened the box and exposed the 7 karat diamond engagement ring.

My eyes widened with surprise and I took my hand from hip and put it out to him. "Yes!" I could no longer hold back my tears as he placed the ring on my finger.

"Okay future Mrs. Wallace. Start planning your wedding." He said as he stood back up and wiped the tears from my eyes before kissing my forehead.

I was waiting for somebody to pinch me because this had to be a dream. My own business and an upcoming wedding, I felt like I was in a fairytale. The constant vibrating of my cell phone ruined my moment. I didn't recognize the number, so I ignored it the first two times it rang. But this caller was persistent, so it must be somebody I know. "Can you turn that down, I'm sorry, I gotta answer this call."

"*Hello.*" I answered with much attitude.

"*My name is nurse Hobbs. I'm calling from lake county hospital looking for Amari Diamond.*"

"*Speaking.*" I straightened my tone when I realized it was an important call.

"*I've been looking for family members of a Monique Odom. Are you her sister?*"

"Yes." I lied although technically I was the only sister she had.

"*She was brought in the emergency room a few weeks ago with a gunshot to the neck. Can you come to the hospital to talk to the doctors about her condition.*"

"*Oh my gosh, yes. I'm on way.*"

~

"Hi, I'm here to see Monique Odom." I arrived at the hospital as quickly as possible after I hung up with the nurse. My nerves were bad the whole drive here as I tried to imagine what happened to her.

"May I see your ID?" The irritated looking hospital receptionist asked.

After writing up a visitor's pass, I removed it from the paper it was attached to and pasted the sticker over my t-shirt. "Thank you." I said to the grouchy woman before heading to Monique's room.

She was sleep with an IV coming from her arm and tubes coming from her nose. I instantly felt sympathy for her as I watched her lay there helplessly fighting for her life.

"Good afternoon. I'm nurse Hobbs. How are you doing today?" The nurse on duty walked in introducing herself.

"I'll be much better when I find out what's going on with Monique."

"I believe I spoke to you over the phone. Are you her sister?"

"Yes, I'm Amari."

"You made it here pretty fast." She giggled as she flicked through the papers attached to the clipboard she was carrying.

"What happened to her?"

"I'll start off by saying this, she's definitely lucky. She fought hard for her life and she's a very strong woman. She was brought in with a gunshot wound to the neck. Doctor says her lung was almost pierced, but it missed by an inch. Thanks to the paramedics quick response she was hooked up to oxygen and her life was spared. The bullet is still lodged in her neck. The doctors don't want to perform the surgery to remove it due to the high risk."

"So, is she breathing on her on now?"

"Yes. She is a fighter. The doctor wants to keep her here a few more days for observation but she should be released after that."

I breathed a sigh of relief and for the first time since I received that call the butterflies stopped moving in my stomach. "Thank God."

"She's gonna need some clothes to come home in because the ones she came in with were soiled with blood." She pointed to a chair near the window that had a clear plastic bag sitting in it. "Those are her belongings, you might want to take them with you because another patient is about to share this room with her and she's been in and out."

I walked over to pick up her bag and sat in the chair. "Okay. I'll make sure I take care of it. Thanks nurse Hobbs."

∼

IT HAD BEEN a month since Tray proposed to me and placed the keys to my business in my hand. Today was the grand opening and I hated that my bitch was still laid up in the hospital and couldn't share this moment with me. The bullet was traveling so the doctors went ahead with the surgery and she was still recovering.

I invited my mother, some of my favorite clients, and a few of my old coworkers from the post office. It was easy to find people to rent the booths out to because the salon was very upscale with the best of everything. Plus, I wasn't charging an arm and a leg for booth rent. I had five hairstylists, one braider, a makeup artist, and two female tattoo artists who were all there as well. We were set to open for business in another hour and we were in the salon celebrating with Champagne and music.

I stood on a salon chair to overlook everyone, "I would like to thank everybody for coming to support the grand opening of Trendy Tresses. Spread the word about this salon because we have the best glam team this city has ever seen. We even have the best female tattoo artists the city of Chicago has ever seen. So, invite your friends, coworkers, sisters, cousins and even your brothers." I grabbed my Belair champagne bottle and shook it up, "Let's toast to a very successful first year." I popped the cork and the bottle exploded with bubbly.

"Here here." My favorite ex-coworker from the post office, Rossi, said raising her glass.

Everybody poured their glasses and toast to new beginnings. I walked over to my station where my mother was mingling with two of the guests admiring the custom designs of my booth.

"I'm still trying to figure out where you get the kind of money it takes to open such a place like this." My mom said as she sat in my stylist chair.

"Ma right now is not the time for this. Can't you just be happy for me and enjoy the moment."

"Everything in my gut tells me something ain't right about this. Ain't no way the post office paid for this." She said as she arched her right eyebrow and sipped her champagne.

She had been questioning me ever since I told her I was gonna finally open my salon. I never told her I quit my job and still hadn't told her about my engagement to Tray. I brought him to meet her one time and she did not the disguise the fact that she just wasn't a fan of his. She said it was something about his energy that she just couldn't vibe with and advised me not to fall for his type.

"Ma, I told you Carver been sending me a lot of money this past year and I've been saving all of it." I said trying to curb her nosiness. Right now just wasn't the time for this and I was not about to let her negative attitude ruin my moment.

"You think I don't know when you lying to me? You're my child and it ain't much you can get past me. Now I came to support you because I love you. But that don't mean I approve of this. I know that damn drug dealing boyfriend of yours got something to do with this. You just better hope he didn't get this with the drug money. Because if the police catch up to him, you can kiss this salon goodbye.

I rolled my eyes to the top of my head and let out a deep breath. I felt myself catching a headache and decided not to even address her about this right now. "Ma that's something else I wanted to announce today. Tray is no longer my man." I pulled my engagement ring out of my pocket and slipped it back where it belonged. I was tired of hiding it from her anyway.

The women that were standing there being nosey and watching our mouths as we conversated gasped when the diamonds from my ring damn near blinded them.

Rossi ran over with her cell phone in her hand. "I'm going live boo. It's time to let the world know how you just bossed up and went from a post office worker to a kept business woman." I was glad she came over and broke up what could have turned into a huge argument between me and my mother.

"Hey yall. I'm coming live from the new hottest salon in Chicago, Trendy Tresses, right off 52nd and Drexel and I'm standing here with the owner, Amari." She said speaking to her facebook followers. She was one of those facebook celebrities who could type the word boo and get a thousand likes. Chick has reached her maximum friend limit and only can get followers. So, I definitely appreciated the advertisement.

"Amari say hi to facebook." She said as she turned the camera around to me.

I let out an awkward, *"Hey facebook."* With the best smile I could muster up. Even though I have a facebook account, social media just isn't my thing.

Rossi kept her live going as she gave her viewers a tour of my salon. I continued with my next announcement. "I would also like to announce my engagement. You're looking at the future Mrs. Wallace." I said as I held my hand up in the air, so everybody could get a view of the ring. My mother for the first time since I could remember didn't have anything to say. She just sat her champagne glass down, picked up her purse and headed towards the exit with a disappointed look on her face. So much for her being happy for me. She didn't even stay for the ribbon cutting. My feelings were hurt and I felt a tear well up in my eye. I no longer cared about the moment, I needed to address this lady once and for all.

One of the hairstylist noticed what was going on and broke me from my thoughts, "Awwwww congratulations." Tiki said purposely stopping me from saying something to my mother. "The engagement and the salon is what most girls dream of and I'm glad you're living yours out."

"Thank you so much."

After everyone was done giving their congrats and the salon was cleared out, we stepped outside for the ribbon cutting. I took the huge scissors and proceeded to clip the red ribbon that surrounded the entrance. "Trendy Tresses is officially open for business." I said as

I gave the ribbon a big snip. Feelings of euphoria filled my veins as I cut that ribbon. I felt like Nicki Minaj, I wish that I could have this moment for life. It was a great feeling to know from this point on, I will never have to punch another clock.

Rossi was the first to leave as she had to go start her shift at work. "I gotta go boo and congratulations again. I don't know how to braid or use a curling iron, but if you ever need an assistant, I'm your girl." She joked as she kissed my cheek and headed out the door.

"I'll remember that and thanks for coming. I really appreciate the support." I reached on my booth and grabbed a handful of my business cards. "Rossi hold up." I walked over to her and passed her the cards. "Give one of these to every hoe at the post office that laughed at me when I told them I would be quitting that job in the near future to open my business."

Clients were already walking in as most of the girls had amazing clientele. I was shocked when three chicks walked in together and the ring leader of the crew, a tall light skinned red head chic, specifically requested that I do her hair. I had been working at the post office full-time so I lost a lot of my clients. I wasn't planning on doing hair today, but she was persistent about the owner doing her hair. All she wanted was a sew-in so I decided to go ahead and take her.

"Hey, thank you for coming to Trendy Tresses." I said as she sat at my station and I draped her with my custom cape.

"I hope you don't take all day, I got somewhere to go, and I got a lot of other stuff to do today." She said as she plopped down in my chair with the nastiest attitude. She reached inside her plastic bag and pulled out three bundles of Brazilian hair and threw them on my station.

"Excuse me, but you did just request me. If you're in a rush, you can feel free to leave." Just that quick she reminded why I hated to deal with certain people. I held my tongue because I was trying to stay as professional as possible. My mother had already pushed every button I have, and I definitely didn't need to be provoked any further.

"Well can we just get started." She said as she took it upon herself to pick up a brush from my booth.

I was getting more irritated by the minute as I watched her brush her hair to the back as if she was about to put it in a ponytail. "Yes, we can. Do you want a full sew in or leave out."

"I think I want a side part with leave out. I'm not sure."

I reached for my comb to get started with the braiding of her foundation. "Okay can you sit back so I can get started." I began braiding and before I could start the second braid she jerked her head away from me and used her feet to swerve the chair around causing the foot rest of the chair to hit my leg. "Damn! Do you gotta braid so tight."

"I have to braid with a little tension so that your style will last." I said still trying to remain professional.

"Well I better still have my edges when I take this shit down." She said rolling her eyes to the top of her head.

The two girls she came in with busted out laughing and one walked towards my station. "Bitch you crazy. Let the damn lady do your hair."

"Ain't nothing funny, you know I'm tender headed."

They started having a whole conversation talking over my head like I was invisible and at that point, the piece of patience I had left melted away. "Okay. Apparently, you are not going to be satisfied with my work, so you can either wait for another stylist to do your hair or leave." I said as I politely unsnapped the cape.

She stood up from the chair and began unbuttoning the blue jean jacket she was wearing. "Is it me or is it hot in here?" She asked the girls she was with who agreed it was hot. She diverted her eyes back towards me. "I want YOU to do my hair." She pointed at me as she emphasized the word. "Maybe if you take that heavy ass ring off your finger you wouldn't be putting so much pressure on my head."

I wrinkled my forehead in confusion, "What my ring got to do with me braiding your hair?" At this point, this bitch didn't even have the option to wait for anyone in my salon to do her hair. And as far as I was concerned she could take her ugly ass friends with her. "You know what, this is going too far. You and your friends need to leave."

"Let's just leave girl. They do better hair up the street anyway." The third troll said as she walked by the door and held it open.

"Wait, I thought they had the best tattoo artist in the city." She said as she took her arm out of her sleeve. "Amari right? You think your artist can do a cover up? Since he's your fiancé now, I don't need to be parading around with his name on me."

My heart jumped to the pit of my stomach as I read the name she had permanently inked on her arm. "Ivory?" I had heard all about her through Monique, but I never laid eyes on her. Tray was adamant about me and her not meeting. I was kicking my own ass because she should have never been able to catch me off guard like this. I knew she was acting like a bitch for something.

"Yea you homewrecking bitch. I'm Ivory. Nice to finally meet you face to face."

"Girl I don't have time for your drama. Can you just leave before I have to call the police."

"I don't have to go anywhere. I helped that nigga become who he is and since he paid for this, technically this my shit too." She nodded her head at the girl standing by the door and the girl that was standing with us started walking towards the back door exit. "As a matter of fact, unless yall want to catch a bullet, yall betta clear this muthafucka out. Tammy, Shevay, Quami," she said and continued calling every employee in the salon by their government names. "I know where all you bitches stay. So, if you even think about calling the police somebody will be at your door before you can hit end on your cell phone." She said as she upped a gun from her purse.

Chaos erupted as everybody started screaming and scrambling towards the door fearing for their lives. I tried to leave too because she was clearly in fucking sane. But her friend who had been conveniently waiting by the door stopped me short of threshold and the next thing I knew I was staring down the barrel of a big ass gun. I looked towards the back and saw thing three with a gun out, I realized then that this shit was a set up. "Everybody can leave except for you." She said backing me back in the salon with the gun in my face.

"Tray ain't even worth all this, you can have his ass." I said as my heart palpitated out of my chest. I wished even more my bitch was here with me. Their little threat would have fell on death ears. She would have never left me here with Charlies angels.

"One of yall go start up the car." She instructed her friends. One left and the other locked the door behind her. "You're right, he ain't worth shit with his lying cheating ass. I just came here to make a point." Ivory said addressing me again.

"You've made your point. I'm not trying be a casualty of some heartbroken bitter-"

"Shut your ass up. I didn't come here to kill you, but I will shoot the shit out of you if you even try to say some more dumb shit."

My armpits started to sweat, and it felt like somebody was beating my chest with a hammer. I don't ever remember being this scared. I've never been in this kind of situation. And if I make it out alive I will never be put in this situation again. I've dealt with a lot of shit from him. But this is the final straw. This bitch on some thin line between love and hate type of shit. "Look Ivory, can you put the gun away so we can talk like two grown women." I pleaded with her.

"Ain't shit we got to talk about. I just came to give you a personal message. As long as you're messing with who belongs to me, your life will be a living hell."

I stood there in shock and remained quiet as she took the gun pointed it at my head with a demonic look on her face. She put her finger on the trigger then quickly turned her gun towards my station mirror and let off a shot. The glass shattered everywhere almost putting my eye out in the process. She then took the gun and knocked down every tool, every hair product and every decoration at my station on the floor. Feeling satisfied with her damage she had her friend to stand guard over me as she repeated the same action at every station. After every mirror was successfully shot up and every booth completely destroyed, her friend took pleasure in using a carving knife to slice up all the chairs including the ones in the shampoo room.

21

TRAY

"Man, we rolled up on that nigga and killed him and his whole crew." Fendi was bragging about how they caught Romell lacking and executed the hit I put out on him. I gave them the address to his crib and told them to put a bullet through that nigga ear.

"Yall sure everything went smooth and everybody was dead?"

"Even if the bullets didn't kill em, the way that crazy possessed mufucka over there chopped off their body parts you betta believe they bled to death." Fendi said pointing at Choppa.

"Ain't nothing wrong with what I do. Mufuckas slaughter animals every day. I'm just a human butcher." Choppa joked.

Me and a few of the guys got together for a meeting. We were at Club Essence in the V.I.P section. "I knew I could count on yall to get the job done." It had been months since the murder of Manny and Romell. Things at the square were back to normal and my gas station was set to open in a few more weeks. I'd saved up enough money to finally get out the game. And since my problems were now taken care of, it was time to pass the torch.

"I have an announcement to make." I exhaled the smoke from my cigar before making my next statement. "I would like to thank all of you for all you have done over the years in Bricksquare. Yall have shown me nothing but loyalty. Fendi and Choppa, yall been under my wing for a while now and it's about time yall put everything I taught yall over these years to good use." As of today, I will no longer be running the square. I'm retiring from the game and I want yall to pick up where I left off. It's a lot of money to be made in those projects and yall got what it takes to keep it going."

Choppa got up from the seat he was occupying and walked over to the table where we had an array of liquor set out. "Aw shit, here I am coming to this meeting prepared to take some more orders and you're telling me I'm the one who will be giving orders?" He poured a shot of D'usse and knocked it back. "This is definitely a cause for a celebration."

"Yea, you and Fendi will control day to day operations and everybody gotta answer to yall from here on out. I already told the connect that he would be dealing with the two of you so I'm gonna give you the contact info after the meeting."

"You know you can count on us." Fendi said with confidence. "Yall hear that right?" He asked the rest of the guys that were at the meeting.

"Naw nigga, our ears clogged up." Taj, the guy who ran the dope building joked.

"Well you betta unclog them muthafuckas. As a matter of fact, pour me a drink nigga. I'm your boss now." Fendi joked back.

"Yall can change the lineup I got and put yall own team together. Of course, yall know yall gotta put somebody in the position yall was in, just choose wisely. Everybody ain't got the heart it takes to do what yall been doing. All I ask is that yall not bring no new niggas in the circle. If they not from the square, they can't break bread at the square."

"Without a doubt." Choppa added. "I wish a mufucka would come on our territory again. And any nigga in the circle that try any snake shit gone see me personally." He looked around the room and looked everybody in their faces waiting for a mufucka to look like they had a problem with his statement. He wanted them to know he meant every word he said and at that moment I felt comfortable with my decision.

"Let's toast to new beginnings." Everybody raised their glasses in the air and all you heard was the sound of glasses clinking together. "Now that we got the important part out the way, let's get some fun started. Taj, go bring in the strippers."

Five minutes later a barrage of half-naked women came prancing through the door. They were in all shapes and sizes. Short, tall, light skinned, chocolate. I even made sure they sent a plus size chick for my boy Choppa because he loved his bbw's. They wasted no time walking up to the guy of their choice and doing what they came to do, make these niggas spend that cash.

"I heard I was requested, who is the lucky guy?" The plus size chic said as she dropped down and did a Chinese split. I ain't even go lie, that shit made my dick jump. I ain't never banged a big girl but she could definitely do this mufucka.

Niggas started throwing money towards her and she was putting on such a good show that she was taking the attention off the skinny strippers. Her ass was so big her thong disappeared in it and even though she was plus size, her caramel complexed body still had a shape.

"Bring that sexy ass over here." Choppa said to her as he pulled out a stack of money. She gathered up the money that was around her, stuffed it in her G-string and walked over to Choppa.

"Aight yall, I'm out. Have fun." I said as I eased out to let the guys enjoy the strippers. I have seen enough naked ass to last me a lifetime.

～

AFTER THE MEETING, I had to pick Ivory up so we could finish planning Lil Tray's super 16 party. We had the youth recreation center in Bricksquare rented out courtesy of Tezza. Ivory hired an interior decorator to put his vision together. He wanted a royal theme and she made sure she went all out for our boy. "You couldn't wait until the weather broke, could you?" She was dressed in cream colored capri pants that were hugging her hips and ass tightly with a cream lace halter. She strutted out with her open toe gold six inch heels looking fine as ever.

"You know I hate the winter time and I'm glad it's over." She said flashing a smile. She went inside her cream and gold colored Gucci hand bag and pulled out a bath and body works lotion bottle. She dabbed it in the palm of her hand and rubbed both hands together before lathering her arms with the lotion. I couldn't help but admire the tattoo on her left arm of my name written inside of a heart with the words "My lifeline" written under it. "Did you call the car lot?"

"Shit. I forgot. I had a busy morning. Call them now and let them know we're on the way." While Ivory called the lot, my cell phone started ringing. "*Hello.*" It was Amari.

"*I finally met your ignorant ass babymama. Where you at?*"

"*I had to take care of some business. I should be back in another hour or so.*"

"*You need to meet me at my salon now. That bitch is crazy.*"

"*I'm on my way to pick up a car for my son party tonight.*"

She started raising her voice yelling into the phone, "*Did you hear what I just said? That crazy bitch just came up here and destroyed my fucking salon.*"

"*She did what?*" I looked over at Ivory who was sitting there with a smirk on her face listening to Amari yell thru the phone.

"*She came up here acting like she wanted her hair did and caught me off guard. That's why I should have known what that bitch look like Tray. But you been keeping her and your son hidden away from me like they some fucking high profile celebrities.*"

"That's the consequences of fucking with somebody man you homewrecking whore." Ivory blurted out jealously.

"*Who is that?*" Amari wanted to know. "*I know you not with that bitch.*"

Ivory tried to blurt something else out and I reached over and smacked fire from her face. "*Look let me deal with her and I'll call you when I'm on my way back.*"

"I knew you was still fucking her. What yall doing together? You told me you was by yourself. Fuck you Tray, marry that bitch since you can't seem to stop fucking with her." Amari spat into the phone before hanging up in my face.

"You got the nerve to put your hands on me over that bitch." Ivory said while trying to throw a punch at me.

It had been years since I put my hands on a woman. I know my mother frowned down on me because she didn't raise me that way. But these bitches be getting out of line sometimes. I grabbed her arm and pushed her into the passenger door so hard it cracked the window "Don't you ever do no disrespectful ass shit like that again. Have you lost your muthafucking mind?" I was so mad I wanted to get out the car and pull her ass out that passenger seat to beat her ass. I gave her ass the look of death to remind her that she didn't want to wake up that Ike Turner in me. "You went too far this time." Ivory made it a point to chase off every chick I ever messed with. And I usually let her get away with it. That's why I've kept her and Amari apart. I knew Ivory wouldn't be able to handle the fact that I actually got someone that I won't allow her to chase off. I just didn't know how the fuck she knew about her or where her salon was located.

"I know you gave her the money for that salon, just like I know you proposed to that bitch." She said calming herself down a notch. "I was enraged and fueled with jealousy." She was crying and yelling at the same time. "What is it about her Tray?" She asked as if destroying the salon was of no importance to her. She put on her seatbelt and folded her arms across her chest. "What has she done for you that I haven't? What she got that I don't got?"

"You been stalking? What the fuck are you some type of private investigator?" This shit was giving me a headache. I didn't even have answers for her questions. I didn't know how to tell her that I never felt the way I feel about Amari about her. It was something I couldn't even explain. "I wish I had an answer for that. You're a good catch Ivory. You're fine as hell and you're a rider. Any man would be lucky to have you."

"For the umpteenth time, I don't want any man. I want you Tray.

All we been through and you gone put this bitch in the position I'm supposed to be in." She was holding her face where I slapped her to soothe the pain from the impact of my hit.

"That don't change our relationship. I'm still gone be here for you."

"You're always just here for me. You know I wanted the title. And I'm not gone stop until I get it. Shit I deserve it."

"I know one thing. If you ever pull some dumb shit like that again, I'm gone make you regret it. This one ain't going nowhere so you might as well get used to her. I let you get away with that shit in the past, but she's different. She's my future wife."

She turned the radio on and we drove the rest of the way in complete silence.

"I WANT to send a special shout out to the birthday boy, Lil Tray. Give it up for him yall." Lil Bibby said after he finished his performance. I'd paid a grip to have him come out because my son is his biggest fan. Lil Tray came on the stage to join Lil Bibby before he made his exit. My son is a spitting image of me. He has braids instead of locs and his hair was freshly braided to the back. He picked out a black, silver, and gold Balmain outfit with some fresh black timbs. He was rocking his Rolex and chain that he'd gotten for Christmas and the lil girls were going crazy over him. I beamed with pride as I watched my boy work the crowd and finesse a few of the young ladies with confidence. The DJ was playing all the music these kids listen to and when lil Uzi Vert song came on they went nuts. I just don't understand this so called hip hop music. If it was up to me we'd be bumping that new Jay Z but this wasn't my party. I walked over to the DJ and grabbed the mic. "We're about to move this party out back for a minute so could everybody start exiting towards those doors." I said pointing to the double doors that led to the back of the center.

Once the whole crowd was outside, I shot Ivory a text telling her to bring the car around. As soon as she turned the corner in a 2018 white BMW with a red ribbon on top of it, lil Tray lost it.

"Yea boy!" He yelled with excitement anxiously waiting for Ivory to put the car in park. "I knew you was gonna get it. You tried to fool me, but I knew it!"

"Damn I wish I had a daddy like Tray. You lucky as hell." One of the boys from the crowd said admiring the ride. The kids were gathering around the car checking out the custom interior. All you could here was oouuus and aahhs coming from the crowd.

"Happy birthday baby." Ivory said as she got out of the car and passed him the keys. "It's all yours."

"Party over." Lil Tray said laughing and snatching the keys from her. "I'm about to take her for a spin."

"Can I ride with you?" A cute lil half-dressed girl said making her way towards the front of the crowd. I wondered was it a coincidence that she was wearing the exact same colors as him.

"Nah, bros before hoes, move around Kaley. He riding with the guys."

"Ain't nobody going nowhere." I said interrupting what was about to turn into an argument. "The party ain't over. Yall can go back inside and finish enjoying yourselves."

"Thanks pops." Lil Tray walked over to me once the crowd dissipated. "I promise you I won't get a scratch on it."

"You don't got to thank me. Just keep doing what you been doing in school, getting good grades and respecting your mother and I'm gone give you the world son." He hugged me and went back inside to continue entertaining his guests.

"Come here Ivory." She was sitting on a fold up chair watching the kids trying to keep her attitude with me going.

"What you want with me? Ain't your hoe somewhere waiting for you?" She said rolling her eyes.

"Why you always gotta bring her up? This ain't about her right now. This about you. You still mad at me?" I walked over to her since she was being stubborn. I stood behind her and wrapped my arms over her shoulders.

"Don't touch me. I need you to stay away from me after this party." She stood up and looked me directly in my eyes. "I need to get over you and move on with my life. And as long as you coming around fucking on me acting like we're in a relationship, I will never get over your ass."

"You gone stop fucking with me when I say I'm done fucking with you. Now fix your face."

"I'm serious, I'm not doing this no more Tray. I'm tired and just like you said, I deserve more than what you've been giving me."

"You right." Nothing I could say or do would change her mood, so I just walked around to the parking lot. "Call me when you make it home."

"I won't be calling you, I'll be okay." She said and walked towards her Range.

"I love you." I yelled to her as she backed her car out.

"Fuck love." She put her car in drive and I could see the tears pouring from her face as she drove off. I turned to walk back inside the center, but the sound of tires screeching made me stop abruptly. A red Cadillac truck came speeding up the street and slammed into the side of Ivory's truck and then sped off.

22

ROMELL

I decided to take Kyra out of town with me until the birth of our child. We found out we were having a girl and she was finally about to push my little princess out. "You need to let them give you that fucking shot."

"I'm not about to let them mess up my back with that shot. I just need some more drugs."

Kyra was going in labor and the pain was kicking her ass. "Aight well stop complaining about the contractions then."

"I wish you could feel this shit then you'll see how easy it is to stop complaining."

Four hours later she had dialated seven centimeters and a team of doctors came in to deliver the baby.

"It's coming I feel the pressure." Kyra squealed out in pain.

The head doctor, a short black woman with blond hair and moles sprinkled all over her face, walked over to Kyra. "Let me check." She said as she put on a pair of rubber gloves. She inserted her fingers inside of Kyra's vagina, "That's the head, she's definitely ready to come out." She instructed the staff to prepare for delivery and everybody took their places. "Give me one big push."

Kyra grunted through tears, "Aaaagghhhh!!"

"Okay stop and take a deep breath for me."

I could see the little head starting to poke out and I immediately became overwhelmed with emotions.

"Push again, this time a little harder." The doctor instructed.

"It hurts."

"She's almost out, push again." Kyra grunted in pain as she pushed for the last time and the babies whole body came slithering out. "Great job. She came out in three pushes. You don't have any rips and won't need any stitches." The doctor said as she was assisted by a nurse with cutting the umbilical cord. "Congratulations. You have a healthy baby girl."

The doctors wrapped her in a blanket and took her over to a warming station where they weighed her and did her measurements. I looked over at Kyra who was being cleaned up by the nurses. The whole sight of the blood and afterbirth was disgusting yet mesmerizing at the same time. She looked exhausted. At that moment I fell in love with her. I already had strong feelings for her, but seeing her push out my baby did something to me on the inside.

"Seven pounds, six ounces and 20 inches long." The nurse said as she walked towards us with the baby. "Who wants to hold her first?"

"I'll take her." My heart skipped a few beats as I looked my little angel in her sweet face. All I could think of is how much I was going to protect my little princess from this viscous world. She looked so innocent and cute. I could already tell that she would be a spitting image of her mother, but she definitely had my ears and nose. "We're gonna name her Princess Royale."

"I think we should switch it around and make Royale the first name since your name starts with an R."

"It'll be like saying royal princess." I contemplated. "I like it, welcome to this crazy world Royale Princess."

"You think I can hold little miss royalty now?" Kyra joked noticing how I was obsessing over her.

I stood up and walked her over to her mother. "I gotta go take care of a few things. I'll be back up here in the morning."

"Where you going? Your baby ain't been in this world for a whole hour yet and you're leaving already. I want to rest, these drugs got me feeling lightheaded."

"I told you I'll be back in the morning. I got a few loose ends I need to tie up before yall come home. We been through enough crazy shit and that can't be going on now that we have a baby to protect."

"Please be careful. We need you." Kyra said as she looked down at the baby then back up to me.

"That's all I know how to be is careful baby."

"Careful enough to not get me kidnapped?" she replied sarcastically.

I kissed my baby then kissed Kyra on her forehead before leaving. "That will never happen again. I just got caught up with the wrong people trying to make money in all the wrong places."

I GOT RIGHT on the road and headed straight for Chicago to take care of my unfinished business. It wasn't even about money no more, it was about revenge. Ever since I found my people dead, I played over in my mind a million times how I would kill the person responsible for it. At this point, nobody was safe, mama, kids, brother, uncle or anybody affiliated with that nigga Tray.

"*I'm about two hours away. Where you at?*"

"*I'm waiting to get my truck from this autobody shop.*"

"*What you getting a paint job or something.*"

"*Nah nigga, I had an accident.*"

"*Damn, I'm glad you ok. I need you for this one.*"

"*I need you more than you need me. I been waiting months to clap back at that nigga Tray. That nigga put a price on my head for some shit I didn't even do. That grimy ass nigga Manny schemed on him and used me as the bait.*" Carver spat into the phone. "*I got here a few days ago and that nigga was having a party at the center in brick square. I circled that mufucka a few times trying to catch that nigga lacking and I lucked up when I saw him and his chick walking and talking. The thing is he turned around and she got in the car and drove off. I slammed into her car at full speed and totaled it."*

"What? I told you to wait for me. Now he gonna know to be cautious. Damn man." I been knowing Carver for a few years now. We met in Iowa thru some lil chicks we was fucking on. He hit me up a while ago and told me he was leaving the Chi for good and needed to get put on. I had just got that big ass shipment from Abel and figured it wouldn't be a bad idea to move work in Iowa too. So, I put him on and he felt he owed me his loyalty. When I reached out to him about making this move on Tray it was a coincidence that he and Manny were the same niggas that chased him to Iowa.

"He don't know who that could have been. He done put out hits and killed so many people he don't know where that message came from. But I know he got it loud and clear though because that car was finito. Plus, you know my truck got tinted windows."

"Who was the chick?"

"Word on the street is it was his babymama, some chick named Ivory."

"Ivory. That name sounds familiar as hell." I tried to recall where I heard that name before but couldn't remember. "

"You know I'm from the square, so I know a lot of the same people he know. We will catch that bitch ass nigga lacking again."

"Now I remember, that bitch tried to holla at me when I used to hold work at that building in the square. She was setting me up then. Well I guess that bitch got what she was looking for. Charge it to the game."

"The game is cold not fair." He replied. *"Hit me back when you make it to the city. My truck ready."*

23

AMARI

I didn't even feel comfortable working in that salon after what Tray skank ass baby mama pulled. So, I closed the shop that day and never went back. He been calling me ever since then and I been ignoring his ass. Today I decided to put him on the block list because his calls were getting on my last fucking nerves. He texted me saying he really needed to talk to me and it was an emergency. But I'm tired of him pissing me off then thinking I'm supposed to act like nothing ever happened. I was starting to regret ever getting involved with him. So, I made it up in my mind that no matter how much I missed his charming personality, generosity, and intoxicating smile, that he would have plenty of time to think about who is more important in his life if I'm who he wants as a wife.

After fixing CJ a bowl of cereal, I got dressed to pick up Monique from the hospital. She was finally being released.

"Mommy I want to go with you." CJ insisted as he sat at the kitchen table chasing the last few fruit loops that were floating in the milk with his spoon.

"Baby I told you I'll pick you up on my way back. Hospitals got too many germs floating around and I don't want you getting sick."

"But I miss auntie Mo."

"She miss you too baby and I promise you she will come see you ok."

"Okay ma."

"Now finish up those cereal so I can drop you off with your granny."

We got dressed and headed for the door. I turned around when I remembered to get Monique's bag and a change of clothes. "Baby run upstairs and look in my closet and get auntie Mo bag out of my closet. It's the only plastic bag in there." He took off running up the stairs and I went through her suitcase and grabbed the first shirt and pants I saw.

"Here mommy." CJ said passing me her hospital bag full of belongings.

I dumped the contents of the bag on the couch and put the outfit inside. Noticing her wallet and cell phone, I grabbed both because I knew she'd want that. As we walked to the car, I powered on her cell phone to see if it needed to be charged. It was at 5% so I hooked it up to my car charger. Before I could pull off the dinging of her cell phone's notifications triggered my curiosity. I swiped the screen and entered the pin number successfully after only two tries. That's how well I knew that girl. She been using the same pin number forever the last two digits of her birth year and the last two digits of mine. Notifications were still coming in but the one that caught my attention was a message from someone she had stored as "That dude." The message was asking her about me, so I scrolled up to read more messages. "Dirty bitch." I yelled aloud as I discovered that "That Dude" is Tray. To learn that my so called best friend came smiling in my face with my mans dick on her breath had my blood boiling.

"Ma who you cursing at?"

"Oh, I'm sorry baby. Nobody." I played it off and put the phone down so I could hurry up and drop him off.

I couldn't drop him off quick enough as I was ready to get to this dirty back stabbing, money hungry bitch. My mama warned me about her a dozen times and now I wish I would've listened. By the time I made it my mother's house I had calmed down and decided I wouldn't confront her at all. I would just cut her out of my life for good and that will hurt her more than anything.

Instead of going to the hospital to pick her up like she asked, I went back home and packed up all her shit in garbage bags and put it in the alley. "Funky bitch." I said aloud to myself as I unzipped her last suitcase. This is where she kept her best and most expensive clothes. I walked into the kitchen and grabbed a canister of used cooking grease off the counter, went back and dumped the whole container in the suitcase. I took her cell phone, wallet, and even the toothbrush she had in my guest bathroom and threw it in the suitcase. "I got your change of clothes of alright." Feeling satisfied with the damage I'd done, I wrote a note and attached it to the zipper. I then took the suitcase to the alley and drained the remainder of the grease on the ground before loading it in my trunk and dropping it off at the hospital.

I don't know why I did this to myself, but I opened up my youtube app and searched for *A Friend of Mine,* by Kelly Price. I drove back home feeling emotional as the music played through my car speakers. "In my heaadddd, in my bed, betrayed by my best friend." I sang loudly as tears streamed down my face. This hurt me more than my breakup with Carver and I never felt more betrayed. I knew she was low down and dirty, but I never imagined for one second that she'd do me of all people. To say I was hurt was an understatement. I was gonna explode if I didn't vent to somebody about my problems. I was tired of putting up this fasad of a strong woman. Tray had brought me to my lowest point. This nigga was just running around sticking his dick in every bitch he could get his hands on. His housekeeper, his babymama, and even my best fucking friend.

Driving up my block, I spotted a shiny red truck parked in my driveway and it broke me out of my deep thoughts. When I got closer, I noticed it had Iowa plates. "Carver? What the hell is he doing here in Chicago?" I said as began wiping the tears from my face.

"What are you doing here?" I asked as soon as I got in the door. He was sitting there drinking a Corona with his leg up on the cocktail table looking awfully relaxed.

"Hey baby mama. Where my son?"

"Did you just hear me? What are you doing here and who told you it was okay to use a key to get in my house?"

"You mean my house? Remember whose name is on the deed." He reminded me.

I made a mental note to start looking for my own place because I don't know who he thinks´ he is. "Just because you bought the house, that gives you the right to barge in unannounced?"

"Technically yes." He said as he squigged down the rest of his beer." Can you grab me another one out the fridge."

I placed my hand on my hip and stared at him like he lost his mind. "Where is your Mexican bitch? I don't fetch beers for you anymore, that's her job. And you just can't be walking in my house like this. I have a man now and we could've been in here fucking for all you know." I said flashing my engagement ring. Even though shit was sour between me and Tray right now, I would never give him the pleasure of knowing.

"I already know you got a man, I see it in your walk. But I know he ain't never been in this house."

"What makes you so sure about that?"

"I asked my son."

I walked over to where he was sitting and punched him in his arm. "Don't be questioning my child about me. Where they do that at? I don't ask him shit about what you got going on with ms Merry maid. And of course, you know I don't bring dudes I date around my son, so you didn't even have to ask him that."

"You bet not." He joked.

"You got a lot of nerve and I just let you take my son with you and your bitch."

"That's different."

"Yea whatever. You still not telling me what you're doing in the city. You told me you wouldn't be back up here for another month."

"Something came up and I had to come on short notice." He said as he got up to go get his own beer. He used the bottle opener to crack it open and walked back in the living room. "I'm leaving tomorrow so I just wanted to see my son since I'm here."

"Oh, you can stop here to see him now? When you bring your girl in town with you, it's like you're forbidden to come here."

"Yea since you won't take him to my mama house. That's something else I wanted to talk to you about. You need to let that shit go Amari."

"Tell your backstabbing mama that." I said rolling my eyes. I didn't feel bad at all for not taking CJ over there anymore. She got to see him when her son came to town to visit him, other than that, I wasn't making no special trips over there anymore and she damn sure couldn't come here.

"Aye, watch your mouth about my mama. I let you get away with that shit you pulled the first time."

"She shouldn't have been in there talking about me with her phony ass."

"Yall gone have to get past that shit for the sake of our son."

I let out a deep breath feeling defeated from the events of my life over this past week. "You're right."

"Now can you go get him from your mother's house so I can see him before I leave."

"I'm tired. You can go over there and get him yourself."

"Can you just go get him right quick? You can take my truck." He said throwing me the keys.

"When you get that truck?" He had a 2018 red Cadillac truck with 26inch rims.

"Not too long ago. You like it?"

"It's alright, a lil too flashy but I guess I'll give it a test drive. I'll be right back." I grabbed my purse off the couch and headed out the door. "I wonder what Arcel would say if she knew you were over her taking naps and shit." I joked before leaving out.

24

MONIQUE

"W hat's today's date?" I was signing my discharge papers because they were finally releasing me. It feels like I been in this fucking hospital forever.

"Today is June 14, 2018." The nurse responded.

"Do you know if my ride is here." Amari should be downstairs by now. The last thing I want to do is sit around downstairs in the waiting area after being laid up in here for damn near a month. I was starting to hate the smell of this place. And if I had to eat one more piece of this fake unseasoned food I'm just gonna die.

"I assume so since someone did bring you a change of clothes. I had the security guard to bring it up. It's right there in the corner. You can go ahead and get dressed then you are free to leave. Don't forget to fill your prescription and make your follow up appointment. We have a pharmacy downstairs and the receptionist can give you a date for your next appointment. Take care Monique." The nurse said before leaving the room."

"I wonder why Amari brought the whole damn suitcase." I said aloud to myself as I bent down to unzip it. The smell of used cooking grease hit my nose as soon as I opened it and my clothes were completely drowned in it. "What the fuck type of shit is this?" I was about to send this hospital into a frenzy over my good threads until I noticed a note with Amari's handwriting:

I knew you were a whore who fucked and sucked for a living. I knew you were a grimy ass piece of shit. But what I didn't know is that you would betray the only person who´s ever shown your snake ass unconditional love. Now I know how you got the money for the down payment on your house. I hope your business meeting with "That Dude" was worth losing me as a friend. Don't worry about coming to my house for the rest of your belongings because I'm sure the alley vultures have sought and destroyed them. Stay the fuck out of my life. If I die don't even show up at my funeral. When you see me in passing don't even acknowledge me. From this day forward, you are dead to me.

P.S,
You never had a reason to be jealous of me because I loved you like you were my sister, but I guess it's a thin line between love and hate.
Amari

SHIT! How could I have been so sloppy and not erase the evidence from my phone of me fucking on Tray. I didn't even realize I had a conscious until now. Amari definitely didn't deserve that from me. I needed to get to my friend and apologize. I just hope she cut Tray off too because I had to let her know that he is the person who killed Manny and damn near took my life. I needed to warn my friend that she can't handle his lifestyle and she needs to get as far away from him as possible. "I'm so sorry friend. Please forgive me." I said as I stared at the letter once last time before tightening my hospital gown and leaving the hospital.

I'm so glad I had on my wig the day Tray followed us to my house and killed him. If he had recognized me he probably would've killed me too. I played dead when I saw him coming and it worked like a charm. I hate how Manny went out but I'm glad my life was spared.

My house had become a crime scene before I even had to the chance to sign the lease. Amari done kicked me out, I don't know where Romell and Kyra are tucked away at and the only other person I could call to get me out a jam was dead. The hospital was not far away from Bricksquare so I decided to walk the six miles. I needed somewhere to lay my head for the night. As I walked the down the street passerby's were staring at me. I was about to snap on this old lady until I realized with my hair braided to the back looking nappy and this hospital gown on, I must've looked like I escaped from a mental facility. I picked up my pace to hurry up and get to my destination. By the time I arrived to the neighborhood, I was drenched in sweat and in desperate need of some cold water. I felt so dehydrated. I walked inside the first building I came to hoping to see a familiar face. Low and behold the face was more familiar than I was prepared for. It was Lorraine Odom, a.k.a. the bitch who pushed me out her coochie. "Well hello Lorraine, long time no see." She was in line waiting to get served. She turned around to see where the voice was coming from and we locked eyes. I wanted to go drag her crackhead ass out of that line and beat her until she told me why she brought me in this world. I was dealt a shitty hand in life and no matter what I've done, things just aren't getting any better. If she was out here using her body for money she could have at least used protection. Thanks to her careless ways I will never have any idea who my sperm donor is. What's even more sad is she didn't even learn from her mistake because Kyra was brought in the world the same way, through prostitution.

"Hey baby girl." She said smiling from ear to ear. She missed me so much she got out that line to embrace me, sike. She spoke and turned around to continue waiting.

I walked out the building to wait for her to come out. As much as I didn't want to, I needed her at this moment. "Where are you off to?" I said as soon as she stepped out the building.

"I got Larry waiting in the car. We're about to go back home and get high." She said as she held up the dope she'd just scored. "Why the hell are you out here in a hospital gown?" She examined me from head to toe and frowned up. "You out here looking bad baby."

I thought to myself she had a lot of nerve standing there looking twenty years older than she should. All those years of drinking, prostituting, and doing drugs had taken a toll on her. "I just got out the hospital. I don't have no clothes, nowhere to sleep, and not a dollar to my name. I need you right now. Can I stay a night at yall house.

She raised up her finger motioning for Larry to wait because he was impatiently honking his horn. "Now you know you can't go with me. I don't know what to tell you. It's barely enough room in that studio apartment for us."

"Just for one night Lorraine. I just need to take a bath, change my clothes, and figure out my next move." I was desperate at this point.

"Look baby, you done survived out here all these years without me. I'm sure you'll figure something out. I gotta go. He's waiting for me."

"You ain't never did shit for me and I ain't never asked you for nothing. My back is against the wall and I have no one to turn to."

She started back walking not interested in my problems. "I don't know what you want me to do. You done chased Amari away. What you do, Fuck her man too? She always been there for you. Won't you go up there with your sister. You know you're an aunt now."

I had followed her to the car still not giving up. But when she announced that I was an aunt, my stomach turned in knots. "I'm a what? You talked to Kyra?"

"Yea, she called my phone the other day to tell me I was a grandmother now. She had a little girl named Royal Princess or some shit like that. She down there in Iowa with some big-time drug dealer named Ro." She said as she hopped in the passenger side of a run down two door Honda Prelude. "Since you took care of her all her life, it's about time she helped you."

"You have her number?"

"Yea." She reached in her bra and pulled a government looking flip phone. She flicked it open and read out her number."

"I don't have a phone right now. Yall got a pen and a piece of paper in there?" I wrote the number down and stuffed the piece of paper inside my shoe. Iowa it is then. Amari got the man I want, Kyra got the man I had, and all I get is the short end of the stick. I'll be damned if they live their happily ever after, it won't happen over my dead body.

25

TRAY

"Didn't you say it was a red truck you saw strike Ivory car that day." Fendi asked pointing to the red SUV that was parked in front of a local Walgreens pharmacy.

I was busting blocks of Chicago with my boys Fendi and Choppa. I had to reach out to them because I hadn't had a good night's sleep since I witnessed the murder of my son's mother. That shit was affecting me in the worse way. "Can you make out the tag?"

"It's definitely not an Illinois plate. I can see that from here." Fendi replied squinting his eyes.

"Get closer to the car." As we drove closer I noticed it had tinted windows and Iowa tags. "That's definitely the one. Pull over."

"Fendi go kill whoever in that mufucka"

Without hesitation, he pulled out his nine, pulled his hoodie over his head, ran up to the truck and emptied his clip in that bitch.

TO BE CONTINUED...

CPSIA information can be obtained
at www.ICGtesting.com
Printed in the USA
LVHW050109180519
618323LV00001B/173/P